THE LOST COMET
by
Stanton A. Coblentz

Author of "THE LAST OF THE GREAT RACE"

As the resources of the earth grew inadequate for its increasing population, scientists began to worry about the "plundered planet" and the dilemma of mankind, which was encroaching on the limits of subsistence. Stephen Rathbone decided to do something more than theorize; he organized a band of intrepid men, and one woman, to set out to find a new, unexplored region of the world which might be developed to serve as a home for future generations.

The band outfitted their dirigible, *The Comet*, and headed for a spot near the North Pole, whose chief features were ice floes and barren wastes. Some friendly Eskimos proved to be helpful allies, but their aid was offset by the depredations of Nature and the mutiny of some of Rathbone's own crew.

In this exciting science fiction tale, present and future merge as daring men attempt to conduct bold new experiments to save civilization.

THE LOST COMET

THE LOST COMET

by

STANTON A. COBLENTZ

WILDSIDE PRESS

www.wildsidepress.com

5

THE LOST COMET

I

"Dear Rodney,

Be at my place tomorrow, eight P.M. Don't be late. For God's sake don't let any other appointment stand in the way.

Yours,

"Steve."

As I glanced at this note in Stephen Rathbone's deliberate, heavy handwriting, I did not know that I stood at the threshold of my life's great adventure.

For more than a year, Steve had been behaving peculiarly. The only son of a fabulously rich father, he and his sister Ada had each inherited a monthly return exceeding most men's earnings for a lifetime. He was, however, no mere playboy; since adolescence, he had been a brilliant scientific experimenter and inventor; and he had used his fortune to build a consummately equipped private laboratory. Otherwise, he would hardly have dared to dream of the experiment with which his name was to be immortally associated.

I was certain that, for twelve or fourteen months, he had been giving his days to some new project. I remembered the huge masses of batteries and electrical equipment which I had seen delivered to his laboratory door; the immense sealed containers marked, "DANGER-OUS: HANDLE WITH CARE." But my questions earned little more than a grunt or growl.

"Get out of here, Rod!" he would snap, his deep-sunk gray eyes taking fire. And he would turn to me with a defiant thrust of his square, almost militant face, which reminded me of a younger, less stocky Churchill's. "Holy thunder! can't a man work in his own lab without being pestered by idiotic remarks?"

That was just like Steve—rough and overbearing at times, but I knew that he meant nothing by it; he had been closer to me than my own brothers ever since our initiation into the same college fraternity nine years before. Just the same, it was cruel to whip up my curiosity, then keep me waiting all those months. And that was why, when I got his message, my heart gave a leap of expectation.

When I reached the penthouse apartment, four

persons were awaiting me.

Rathbone, as he leapt up to seize my hand, threw a rueful glance at the large electric clock, which registered 8.02. At his side, heartily grasping my other hand, stood aviator and explorer John Norwood: a broad-shouldered six-footer, with oversized features in a large, hearty face, a hooked, piratical nose, and deep blue eyes that could be as soft and ingenuous as a child's, yet had a habit of scanning the distance with an eagle glint.

"Good Lord, Rodney," he greeted me, almost knocking the wind out of my body with a cordial slap on the back, "don't you know you're late—all of a hundred and twenty seconds? Steve here has been fuming and raving!"

As he planted another slap on my back, the room shook with the thunder crashes of his mirth.

Meanwhile a third figure had stepped forward. In an insinuating, catlike way, Alan Allenham projected himself between Norwood and me and extended a soft, neatly manicured hand with the firmness of a sponge.

"Glad to see you, Farnsworth," he drooled, his Bostonian accent oozing affectation. And I too said I was glad—which, heaven help me, was a plain lie. Clearly, however, I was prejudiced; for he was what the world would call attractive, with his well-groomed form of slightly more than average height; and his smooth, rounded features, unmarked by time or trouble.

But it was not he that held me. When I turned to the fourth member of the party, it was as if none of the others existed.

Even now I can see Ada Rathbone as she was in those days: the reedy, athletic form; the eyes that were liquid blue globes of laughter; the bobbed light-brown hair that was always getting disordered over the wide forehead; the gently whimsical manner that seldom seemed far from mirth; the rippling smile that moved me like music. Yes, like music; sometimes for days after seeing her I was a haunted man. Yet we had been good friends, but no more; an almost penniless laboratory technician, I had put a gag in my mouth whenever I thought of the difference in our fortunes. . . . And so one fine morning I had received the bitterest shock of my life. Out of all her suitors, her choice had fallen on Alan Allenham!

Even so, her spell for me remained, as subtle, as bewitching as ever; I could hardly take my eyes off the changeable rose tints of her face.

"Ready, Rod?" Rathbone threw at me in his husky bass, after we had all taken seats. "Might as well begin!"

"Begin what?"

"Something as secret as Tut-ank-hamen's tomb, from the looks of things!" snorted Norwood, passing the cigarettes.

Rathbone lifted one blunt, stubby-fingered hand imperiously, somewhat as if it held an invisible rod.

"This last year," he opened, with characteristic explosiveness, "I've been engaged in some important research—most important in my life. If it comes out right, it'll change all human life on this planet. Maybe that's a small claim, folks."

"Well, I wouldn't exactly call you a blushing rosebud of modesty," commented Norwood, throwing me a meaningful wink.

"Blushing rosebuds have nothing to do with scientific fact!" boomed Steve. "That's what I've called you here about—scentific fact—yes, fact that may transform the planet. You, John, should be the last to scoff. You put me up to it."

"Me?" roared Norwood with mock indignation. "Ye gods! So I'm called here to bear the blame?"

"That remains to be seen. If you remember, a little more than a year ago you came here, after an Arctic expedition—"

"Just listen to him, folks!" Norwood broke in, his counterfeit fury rising. "He asks if I remember—*if* I remember—after I'd had the meanest deal of my life, lost my plane, and been marooned five weeks on an ice floe."

"But that's not all," Steve hastily went on. "Don't you remember how you were brimming with enthusiasm—hot, overflowing enthusiasm for the possibilities of the North?"

"If you think I have any hot enthusiasm for riding another ice floe—"

Half-suppressed smiles flashed between Ada and me.

"Maybe you've forgotten," Rathbone interrupted. "What you said was simply this: scientists are worried about 'our plundered planet,' and mankind encroaching on the limits of subsistence. You mentioned this, and said you wished those scientists would cast an eye at the Arctic. All in all, you estimated, thirty or forty thousand Eskimos are living in an area as large as Europe. So there's a task for some engineer of the future—to turn that frosty wilderness into productive territory!"

"You bet there is a task!" agreed Norwood.

"Now the Arctic," Rathbone continued, "is in the world's most strategic location—at the threshold of three continents. What's more, it's not half so hostile to life as some of us suppose."

"True," acknowledged Norwood. And he lifted his eyes with that characteristic far-away look of his, and seemed to be staring across glacial barrens and iceberg seas. "The climate for two or three months a year is really all we'd have to counteract. In many places, the soil is good enough, as you can see from the grass and wildflowers during the brief warm season. If we could raise the average temperature in favored localities even a few degrees, we could prolong the summer and harvest wheat and other hardy crops. After all, North Dakota and Manitoba in January aren't so far behind the Arctic."

"Exactly what you said before, John. So I put two and two together, and decided that what we needed was some way to control the air currents or regulate the summer temperature. That's what I've been working on folks. Naturally, I didn't want to talk till I had the proposition licked."

Suddenly we all sat up in our seats.

"Now that I know just where we're at," he went on, with an assurance that I marvelled at, "I've summoned you all here on a project that may drain the last energies of us all."

"Hear the man! Just hear him!" burst out Norwood. "What in blazes does he think we are? The U. S. Congress?"

"The U. S. Congress never had any nut like this to crack. Listen, folks! Polar lands can be reclaimed *now* —we don't have to wait till the year 3000!"

"Found a way, have you, to make the ice floe bloom as the rose?" Norwood gibed.

"No, only a way to make frozen tundra sprout thriving towns!"

All of us had been petrified into attention. Even Allenham had thrown off his habitual bored nonchalance. Ada, her hands clasped together in her lap, beamed at her brother, who went on with an enthusiasm that made every word coruscate.

"As John has brought out, the problem is to control the temperature. If the ocean or the streams or lakes in any particular locality could be heated sufficiently—"

"What about atomic power?" I broke in.

"That power might be the soluton—if the world wasn't so busy trying to make bombs. No, it would be years, decades, before we could build the necessary plants. However, we don't have to wait that long. No, thank the Lord! there's another source of energy right under our feet! One millionth part of it would run all the world's dynamos."

"Heaven help him! His insanity is progressive!" mocked Norwood. "Now hear what he's after! Wants to tap the earth's internal heat!"

"Take things easy, John. You've guessed it, all right—I'm going to bore down into the very bowels of Dame Nature."

To me, as I look back, the surprising thing was not that Steve made this claim. The surprising thing was the definiteness of his assertion.

"Very simple, Steve," came Norwood's voice, with a sarcastic edge. "All you have to do is dig through maybe a thousand miles of rock and iron."

"What makes you think so?" Rathbone challenged; and went on with thundering gusto, "Ever been down in a deep mine? You know how the temperature climbs as you descend. At half a mile, the heat is infernal. The average rise in temperature throughout the world is about one degree Fahrenheit for every fifty or sixty feet you descend—allowing, of course, for differences caused by the materials of the earth's crust. Please note that this means a gain of nearly a hundred degrees a mile."

"So how many miles do you think you're going

down?"

"Not very many! Even in the Arctic, less than three miles should bring us to the boiling point of water. My plan," continued Rathbone, "is to make a bore that will take us down till the temperature reaches 212 Fahrenheit. The excavations, of course, will be by mechanical means exclusively. But so as to make it possible for workmen to descent, I'll provide heat-resisting asbestos clothing and a continuous pumped supply of cool air. The actual power will be generated electrically."

"Lord preserve us!" howled Norwood. "Will there never be an end of miracles? Now the man is supposing there are power houses scattered all over the Arctic!"

"I'll provide my own power house!" bawled Rathbone. "But wait, you hide-bound sceptic! I've got something concrete. Want to see a model of the project?"

On a swift impulse, Steve had started toward the elevator. The rest of us trailed after him; and were soon on our way to the basement laboratory twenty-two stories below.

II

Through an evil-smelling room littered with test tubes, beakers, crucibles, and bottles of vari-colored fluids, Steve enthusiastically led the way; then across a compartment crowded with electro-magnets, motors, pipes and batteries, into a large room baking in a hot-house heat, where an iron basin, about ten feet square, glittered with a pool of water. At the further end, beyond a long glass partition, was one of the queerest contrivances I had ever seen.

Eight or ten feet tall, it showed two perpendicular shafts reaching down through rock and earth; the wider about as thick as a broom handle; the other considerably narrower. In the smaller shaft, an elevator-like contraption dangled from a wire halfway to the bottom; the main tube was featured by a tangle of lesser tubes, each thinner than a pencil, and several extending to its base, where they were lost amid coils and boilers. In the central bore I noted a number of balconies and valve-like arrangements; the latter, distributed at intervals along its sides, were room-shaped, and showed tiny images of men at work.

For a moment we all stared in silence.

"So?" Norwood finally broke out. "What in Pete's name is it, Steve?"

"A toy to change human life on this planet! Of course you won't believe me, John—but notice what I represent here. The scale is about an inch to two hundred feet. The larger shaft is for the machinery; the smaller is for men to descend in. Notice how the pipes from the main shaft are filled with water from the lake"—he paused to indicate the pool in the iron container—"and how electric pumps force it out the underground boilers, then back into the lake."

"Oh, I see!" I burst out. "You plan to take the cold water from the lake, send it underground till the earth's internal heat raises it to boiling, then return it to the lake, whose temperature will go up so many degrees that the climate of the surrounding country will be changed."

"By thunder, Rod, you've said it!" shouted Steve, giving my hand a congratulatory clasp.

"Still," I objected, "you'll have to heat enormous quantities of water to keep the temperature from dropping as fast as you can raise it."

"Don't I know that? But remember, water holds its temperature much longer than air. A lake of six or seven square miles, with a rapid enough turnover of water, should control the temperature of twenty square miles of land. Look! I've got other materials over there," Rathbone hurried on, pointing to a closed door. "For instance, a model of the apparatus to generate electricity from pressure of the ice pack. You see, the ice, as it shifts about under the winds and tides, gets up terrific pressure—pushes itself into all sorts of monstrous ridges and hummocks. Isn't that so, John?"

"I'll say it is. Sometimes, too, it cracks with a roar like TNT."

"So the idea came to me of hitching this titanic force. The supply's inexhaustible. Shall I show you the model?"

Three of us had already started toward the closed door, at which Rathbone had flicked a finger. But Allenham put up a detaining hand.

"No, thanks," he dissuaded, in oily tones. "Don't trouble yourself, Steve. We've seen quite enough to understand everything."

"Nothing like having a quick grasp!" Rathbone snapped, with a disappointed look. "Well, then let's get back upstairs. I still haven't put my proposition."

As the elevator door closed, Ada could not keep back her enthusiasm. "I think Steve's on the trail of a wonderful idea, don't you?" she bubbled over, her eyes brilliant.

"Yes, indeed," Allenham took up, in his best measured drawl. "So wonderful he'll end up by making Eskimos of us all."

To me there was something unbearable about Allenham's slow, supercilious, too carefully enunciated speech; and, besides, I didn't like the way he kept on making eyes at Ada.

Back in the penthouse, Rathbone strode to and fro, arms folded Napoleon-like.

"Now as to the plan: I'll pick some section of the North, preferably far from inhabited areas; and will settle there with a good-sized force of men and all necessary equipment."

"Glorious Lord! he's at it again!" Norwood intruded. "What's that old saying about 'Where wise men fear to tread'? Now listen, Steve, you've got the most admirable nerve, but there are some little gaps in what you know about the Arctic. You must think streamlined trains travel there on regular schedules. Why, don't you know that going even by vessel is as dangerous as a parachute jump, and impossible in many places? For ground transport we still have to rely pretty much on dog teams."

There was condescension, almost pity in the glance which Rathbone levelled at his critic from beneath his bushy brows.

"The trouble wth you, Norwood, is that you haven't any imagination. What makes you think I'm still living in the dogteam age? The real way to conquer the Arctic is by air."

"You're telling me?" thrust back Norwood. "Maybe I didn't try it, and have ages to think things over on that lovely ice floe? No, never again! Besides, you'd need a Berlin air lift."

A silence descended, and Rathbone went on:

"I'm with you when you say no ordinary plane—not even a fleet of them—would really serve. My plan is to go by dirigible. Maybe you've forgotten, but many years ago the *Norge,* under Amundsen and Ellsworth, successfully flew across the Pole."

"Yes, and later," Norwood hastily added, "the *Italia,* under Nobile, also flew across the Pole—and was dashed to splinters on the way back. Besides, Steve, it's easy to go to the Government and charter a dirigible."

"Again, you're lacking in imagination, John. Why charter a dirigible? I'll make one."

Allenham, his polished billiard ball of a face widening into a grin, laughed aloud. Norwood looked amused and incredulous. Only Ada was staring up at the speaker with an assured, calm faith.

"I'll make a dirigible," Rathbone rushed on, "of an entirely new type. Lighter-than-air machines have never been quite satisfactory, for they've been filled either with helium, which is rare and costly; or hydrogen, which is in danger of exploding. But why use any gas at all? A vacuum, obviously, would be lighter and more satisfactory. It happens that, for several years, I've been playing around with a vaccum type of dirigible, with a thin, tough envelope of a non-inflammable magnesium alloy. I've made small models that drift in airlike balloons. A full-scale machine is now being built."

Steve paused, and met our speechless glances with triumph on his square, strong face.

. "I won't bore you with details. In time, you'll see for yourselves. The point is that I expect to be ready to start sometime next summer. I'll want everyone's cooperation—believe me, I'll need it!"

"You certanly can count on mine, Steve!" cried Ada,

her clear, musical voice vibrant with enthusiasm.

"I'm with you, too!" I joined in. And, simultaneously there came Allenham's bored drawl. "If you're in need of any capital—"

"Thanks. Don't need any—" Rathbone cut him off, bluntly.

Only Norwood had remained silent.

"Well, how about you, John? Maybe you can't support any such harebrained scheme?"

An ingratiating smile flowed over Norwood's face. The deep blue eyes blazed. "Well, it may be harebrained," he acknowledged, "but that puts it just in my line!" And then, his voice rising to thunder, "You know I'm not the man to let a pal down simply because he's gone crazy. Besides, I'm getting plumb tired of civilization. So take out your pencil, Steve, and put me down for a reserved seat on that dirigible."

III

Ten months later, Rathbone's dirigible *The Comet* stood at anchor upon a New Jersey field.

The interval had been hectic. The whole period remains in my memory as a blur, in which conference followed upon conference, decision upon decision, with bewildering speed.

The first question was that of the site for the experiment. Originally we had thought of Greenland or Baffin Land, but Norwood made a more tempting recommendation.

"Since we're to begin with a small area, I'd suggest an island," he remarked one evening when we were all comfortably sprawled about Rathbone's living room. "On my last expedition I sighted one which maybe no human foot has ever touched. You won't find it on most maps; yet it's twenty or thirty miles long, and possibly half that wide. In its center there's a partly frozen lake about as large as Upper New York Bay."

I could see something kindle under Rathbone's beetling brows. "Where is the island?" he demanded.

"Almost at the top of the world." Norwood paused reflectively, then mentioned a point somewhere between 175 and 180 degrees West Longitude, and between 80 and 82 degrees Northern Latitude. "Got a map handy?"

A moment later, we were all poring over an atlas.

"See, it's halfway between Wrangel Island and the Pole," Norwood stated, indicating an unmarked point on the blank blue expanse between the easterly tip of Siberia and northern Spitsbergen. "Remember Wrangel Island? It was the objective of the ill-fated expedition sponsored years ago by Stefansson. Four white men and an Eskimo woman were left there for two years. In the end the only one found alive was the Eskimo."

"Sounds encouraging," remarked Allenham, reaching for a cigarette.

"Well, that's a matter of opinion," Norwood retorted, as he rose to his majestic six foot two and began stalking about the room. "As for me—I'm just the sort of darn fool that finds such a place appealing. Of course, not everything is going to be roses and honey. I hope you won't be scared off by the name I've given the place."

"What do you call it?" asked Rathbone with a smile. "Desolation Reef?"

"No, Icy Isle."

After some further discussion, during which Allenham cast the one dissenting vote, we agreed on Icy Isle as our tentative destination.

The choice of a site was, however, the least of our problem. I had never before realized Rathbone's skill as an organizer. He had to obtain a complete outfit for a party of seventy-five; to provide condensed and varied food for a year; to supply the necessary fur clothing; to furnish oil and gasoline for the dirigible, and medicines for the men, as well as snowshoes, skis, weapons, ammunition, icepicks, and other tools, along with scientific apparatus, barometers, thermometers, field glasses, surgical instruments, and—most important of all—the dynamos, batteries, wires, and electric bulbs, heaters, pumps and drills essential for the experiment, along with a vast quantity of pipes, screws, boilers and other metallic contrivances, and the parts of our prefabricated houses.

Of course, we realized that this paraphernalia would be too much for one dirigible. "I'll pack the airship with all it can carry," Rathbone decided, "and load all the other material on a steamer bound for Nome. The dirigible, making as many round trips to that point as necessary, will bring us all our supplies."

"God preserve us!" derided Norwood, after listening with a skeptical smile. "Know what you're asking? Your dirigible, even if it keeps to the direct course, will have to cover twenty-four hundred miles each round trip between Nome and Icy Isle. Maybe you haven't any dea of the head winds it'll have to buck?"

"The dirigible," smiled Steve, with that impenetrable assurance which never for a moment left him, "will be built to laugh at head winds."

The construction of the airliner itself was, naturally, one of his chief concerns. Daily he spent hours in the steel works which had been given the contract, examining every bolt and rivet in the whole great mechanism. "One defective screw, and we may end on the rocks," he would explain. And I was more and more impressed, especially when, after several months, I saw the half-finished skeleton of the ship, whose 936-foot cigar-shaped frame loomed like a man-made mountain.

"She looks fine," I commented, noticing the amount of metal that was used. "But how are you going to make her fly?"

Rathbone laughed. "She'll have to fly. Her walls,

being of a specially prepared magnesium alloy, are both tough and light—less than a quarter of an inch thick—yet they'll have nothing to fear from atmospheric pressure or gales. The inner partitions will be still thinner—of an airproof special parchment. Electric suction pumps will drain the air from the one hundred and twenty-two compartments."

"How much will the machine weigh, complete and unloaded?"

"About ninety-eight percent of the specific gravity of the air."

A misgiving assailed me. "Good Heavens, man! When loaded, she'll be much heavier than air!"

"Don't you think I've calculated all that, Rod? Remember, birds are many times heavier than air, and so are airplanes. The buoyancy generated by the flight more than overcomes the excess weight."

"But what if you have motor trouble?"

"The dirigible will have six engines." Steve cut me short with an emphatic wave of the hand. "Three would keep her afloat."

Rathbone now gave himself to selecting his personnel. And again Norwood's advice was invaluable.

"Take only blonds. They'll hold out better through the winter darkness. Also" —and this struck me as

peculiar, since Norwood himself was a large man—
"pick the small wiry fellows. They eat less, are easier
to haul around, and get about quicker, particularly
crossing thin ice."

"We'll put that in our ads," gibed Rathbone. "Only
experts in crossing thin ice need apply."

"Another thing," went on Norwood: "better hire
one or two Eskimos at Nome, including Eskimo women
to repair the clothes. In addition, I'd advise you to bring
along two or three dog teams and experienced drivers.
Probably you'll never need them—still, you can't tell."

Rathbone smiled and mumbled something about
"not getting cold feet." But he did everything that
Norwood advised.

Months later, we had enlisted most of the personnel;
which would include a physician, Dr. Joseph Straub,
and two scientific assistants; one or two engineers; a
dirigible pilot and crew, including Captain Knowlson and Chief Engineer McDougal; about fifty laborers;
two Eskimo women; and two drivers with dog teams.
Then, within a few weeks of our departure, two not-
able additions were announced.

One evening when I visited Rathbone's apartment,
his broad, square executive's face was crossed with a
troubled smile. As I sank into the sofa across from

him, I observed the furrows under his eyes.

"Lord, Steve," I chided, "you could pose for a picture of Atlas bending under the world's weight."

He paused, shrugged and flung both hands up in a gesture of hopelessness.

"Come on, now! What's troubling you, Steve?"

"Oh, nothing much," he denied, rising and ambling over to a table, where he idly turned the pages of a huge *Geodosy of the Arctic.*

"You know, Rod," he confided, "a man can lick the scientific features of a job, but just as if some mocking little devil stood by, he can be balked right in the heart of his own family."

"What do you mean—heart of his own family?"

Rathbone turned from the table. A glare came from beneath his bushy lids.

"Now, Rod," he said suddenly, "there's no one in the world I think more of than Ada. But our expedition is no place for a woman—not a white woman, who's always had every comfort. Ada, however, thinks differently. We've been arguing it out for months. It doesn't do any good to refuse her—doggone that girl, she's got the Rathbone iron in her make-up!"

I must admit that I was not appalled at the prospect of Ada's company. "What does Allenham say about it?" I asked.

"What do I care what that ass says? He reminds her, of course, they were going to be married this summer."

"And she—she wants to put it off?" I stammered, an unreasonable hope flickering up within me.

"Yes—until after their return from Icy Isle."

"*Their* return? Mean to say *he's* going too?"

"What else do you think I mean?"

Lowering his voice and coming to me with the old confidential, ingratiating manner, Steve continued, "Between you and me, Rod, he's putty in her hands."

"Why don't you dissuade him?"

"Maybe you'd like to try, Rod—with Ada on the other side of the fence, leading him round like a monkey on a string!"

He paced over to the window, where he stood with hands folded behind him, gazing down at the motor-crowded street.

"Go on, Rod," he proceeded in his heavy burring voice, "call me the prize blockhead for ever taking Allenham into my confidence. But you know I couldn't help myself. Lord! you should have heard Norwood laugh when I told him Allenham was going!"

I too could have laughed. However, I could almost endure Allenham, now that Ada was to join us.

IV

"Well, boys, everything ready?"

"Yes, sir, it's all shipshape."

His face dripping perspiration in the July sun, his hair disheveled on his hatless head, his broad, moderately tall figure racing back and forth, Rathbone supervised the final loading of *The Comet* and the embarkation of her passengers. Before him the dirigible stretched, an enormous silvery white apparition which gleamed and sparkled in the sunlight, different from any airship previously flown. She did not, for example, have any "gondola" or other appendage; instead, an immense opening forward, shaped like a shark's mouth, contained accommodations for the passengers, while similar compartments to the rear served as storage rooms for the freight.

Cheering, waving flags and blaring horns, the crowd

streamed about our anchorage. But most of us had small thought of the tumultuous thousands. I remember the jubilant look in Ada's clear blue eyes; I remember how Allenham slunk forward catlike, with stooped shoulders and a cowed expression. I remember, also, Norwood's exhilaration as he stalked back and forth, slapping old friends on the back and startling us all with the explosions of his mirth. Also, I noticed that Rathbone, when he ordered the gangplank lifted and the machine began to shudder and the propeller blades started to whirl, wore a stern, set expression.

With a jerky, horizontal motion we moved along the runway, our enormous bulk supported on a dozen little motorcycle wheels. Then, automatically the wheels folded beneath us, and we were darting with express-train speed above the housetops.

Forty-eight hours and thirty-five minutes after embarking, we set foot on the soil of Nome. There we replenished our supplies of oil and gasoline, and took on our Eskimos and their dog teams, our fur clothing, and several light Eskimo boats or "kayaks" for navigating ice-littered seas.

Then, after a few hours, we had left Nome on our final lap and were crossing northern Alaska. On every side, we could see drifting and broken ice floes, here and there parted by long lanes of open water, or varied by some castle-like berg; while a ghostly whiteness had settled over all things except where the ice, beneath the pale beams of the midnight sun, glinted emerald green or sapphire or shone with a cold, iridescent light.

And now a change came over our spirits. Our bantering mood deserted us. Norwood, the most cheerful of us all, spent hours at the glass enclosure of the promenade deck, his deep blue eyes grave with a falcon sternness. Ada, staring a little wanly at those wide, fantastic wastes, seemed depressed; as I looked at her slim, girlish form, she somehow seemed frailer, more in need of protection than ever before. As for Allenham—he had become gloomy, almost morose, "Beastly place," he would mumble, pointing to some fortress-shaped floating ice tower. "If I ever see Central Park West again, I'll get down on my knees and give thanks."

But it was Rathbone who showed the most disturbing change, Once, as he stood alone at the rail, I caught him gazing toward a low, red-misted sun with a disconsolate look on his square, rugged face, his lips straightened into severe lines. For a moment, by a weird fancy I wondered if his first glimpse of northern seas had given him some forewarning.

"Not letting the north get into your blood, Steve?"

I asked, swinging one arm heartily about his shoulders.

A moment passed in silence.

"No, no, not that," he answered, in the deliberate tones of one who seeks to clarify things for himself. "Can't say I exactly expected palm groves and coral the responsibility I've piled on my back. Seventy-five lagoons. But maybe I'm at last beginning to realize human lives!"

He hesitated; fell into a drearier manner. "Then there's the problem of Icy Isle. After all, Rod, we've made pretty much of a plunge in the dark. If I've fallen into any false reckoning—well, I can't afford that. Simply can't afford it."

"Can't afford it?"

His tones grew even more solemn.

"Might as well take you into my confidence, Rod. This expedition is costing a blamed sight more than I'd figured. *The Comet* alone gobbled up millions. And when it came to investing my entire fortune—"

"Your entire fortune?"

"Not only that, but the better part of Ada's in the bargain. I fought like a wildcat to stop that—but she has a will like a brick wall. Naturally, it's only a loan, which the expedition should pay back; but just the same—"

Suddenly he gave himself a hearty shake, like a dog that has been out in the rain.

"Lord! What am I talking about?" he boomed. "Guess those infernal icebergs are turning me goofy, making me lose my nerve. Of course everything is going all right! I've got it all figured out, down to the tiniest detail. We're going to lick Icy Isle—fact is, we've got it half licked already!"

Several hours later one of the crew, staring through binoculars across the white waste, let out a triumphant "Land ahoy!"

We all rushed to the deck, where we took turns peering through the glasses. I could hardly wait for my chance; but when I had adjusted the lenses, my sensation was one of disappointment. Many miles across the frosty wilderness, a bald snow-capped ridge was faintly visible, so vague in the distance that it might have been another iceberg.

"Icy Isle! Icy Isle!" we all yelled, running back and forth and jubilantly shaking hands. All, that is, except Allenham, who sat scanning the distance with a bored expression; and Norwood, who stood peering through the binoculars with a long earnest scrutiny.

"I'm a crazy loon if you're not right! It *does* look like Icy Isle!" he finally announced. "Guess I won't ever forget the mountain's peculiar shape—its queer broken ridge, like a rough face. You know what ungodly fancies a man forms in parts like these; that's probably why it always looked just like a devil to me—a devil with its mouth wide open in a mocking smile."

These words, strangely, touched some ancient core of superstition in me, and I shuddered. Yet Norwood's impression did spring out of something more than imagination. We were still twenty or twenty-five miles away when the field glasses plainly showed us the snow peak, its eastern slope riven by dents and fissures that gave it the grotesque semblance of a human face. And that face was carved wth a long, sharp nose and a gaping mouth, so that it did remind one of a laughing devil.

Immediately, at my suggestion, we christened the mountain "Devil's Peak."

Now, as we bustled to seize caps and coats, bedlam arose among us. Captain Knowlson was thundering orders to the crew, the crew was scuttling back and forth; most of us were roaring jests and congratulations; even Allenham smiled as he pointed to a carpet of undulating green and brown that stretched from the beach two or three miles toward the rocky spurs of the foothills.

"Gorgeous! Simply gorgeous!" enthused Ada, indicating the hills, with their fantastic seams and black canyons varied by the glare of snow patches and glaciers, behind which, like a great hood, jutted the spectral white of Devil's Peak.

A few minutes later we were soaring above the island. Round and round in ever-narrowing circles we floated, while Captain Knowlson anxiously searched for a landing place on the rolling fields of lichen and moss. Gradually we were sinking; and at length the commander, finding the desired spot, snapped out the order to descend.

Perhaps, in the excitement, the order was executed a little too abruptly. The next second, as the whirring of the propellers died out, we were hurtling earthward with frightening speed, and struck with a thud that sent most of us sprawling face downward.

Oaths, groans, and screams came from dozens of lips. And the vessel, quivering like an injured live thing, jerked along the ground for a few feet and rattled to a halt.

V

With a dizziness in my head and a dull pain in my side, I dragged myself out of the cabin door.

At the same time, from the deck at my side, an energetic figure sprang to life regardless of the blood that streamed from a cut lower lip; dashed across the deck; threw open a little door; and was gone.

The rest of us, bruised but not badly hurt, followed in a shoving, white-faced mob. Our leader, with grim, taut features, moved slowly about the rear of the airship, pausing every few seconds to rap against the metal walls.

After each rap he grunted with relief. But upon covering two or three hundred feet, he paused and did not tap; paused and stood staring fixedly at a great boulder which, projecting several feet above the soil, had grazed the vessel's stern. There were four or five deep dents where the rock had struck several compartments.

While the blood still streamed from his cut lip, he began uneasily to explore each of the dents. His militant face reminded me of some embattled general's as he tapped from time to time, and from time to time put one ear to the metal walls.

By now Norwood was towering beside Rathbone, along with the equally tall, slimmer form of Captain Knowlson, and the slight frame of Chief Engineer McDougal. These silently joined in inspecting the damaged compartments.

After a few minutes, the captain and chief engineer seemed to relax.

"Well, could have been worse," diagnosed Knowlson. "Metal's knocked out of shape a bit, but no air's getting in."

"Thank heaven!" exclaimed Rathbone.

But Norwood, who had been standing with one ear against a compartment, motioned secretly to me. His eyes were bleak. "Just listen!" he invited.

I listened attentively. Did I only imagine that low sucking sound?

In Norwood's glance the truth was alarmingly plain.

"Oh, well," he tossed off, "I never was in an expedition where some blamed thing didn't happen. After all, Rod, it's only one compartment."

"One too many!"

"Hey, you!" he called to McDougal, who was edging near. "Come and see what you can hear. I think this compartment's punctured!"

But McDougal, after listening for minutes, declared that he heard nothing. And Knowlson, Rathbone and others, listening in turn, agreed that there was no sound.

"Guess you're wrong this time, John," Rathbone finally pronounced. "Not that I hold it against you—it's deuced easy to imagine things under these strained conditions."

"Well, maybe I *am* suffering from a diseased imagination," Norwood retorted. "Still, if you'll take my advice, you'll look for that leak and fix it while there's still time."

But amid the excitement of reaching Icy Isle, we had other things to do besides tediously seek out a probably non-existent leak.

Nevertheless, our mishap did require an explanation. "Afraid we hit some sort of air pocket," I heard Captain Knowlson remarking to Rathbone. "Working at a quarter normal capacity, the engines should have held back our descent sufficiently, just as at Seattle and Nome."

"Don't forget we've more baggage abroad now. But

heaven be praised it wasn't worse!" Rathbone replied, as he dabbed at his bleeding lip.

Now for the first time we could really look around us. Ada did an impromptu dance of joy on the lichen-covered soil; the rest of us began to ramble about excitedly. After all, the Arctic was not so unfriendly! True, icebergs drifted about the sea, and the white dome of Devil's Peak and the nearer white of a glacier looked stern and forbidding; but the breeze was gentle, and I had known more biting cold in July as far south as San Francisco.

During most of that day, however, we were too busy for jubilation. Hundreds of tons of cargo had to be un-loaded, so that the dirigible might fly to Nome for further supplies; the vessel had to be moored, and her engines tested and oiled; and we had to erect permanent shelters out of materials carried in the ship's hold.

No Eskimo snow huts for us! Rathbone had devised prefabricated houses, the inner walls constructed of a thin layer of steel lined with concrete, the outer walls insulated with a light, fibrous product of asbestos and wood pulp. "It's one of the poorest heat conductors ever discovered," Rathbone explained. "Just what we'll need when the blizzards start howling down from the Pole."

Within six or eight hours, the houses stood in place, seventeen in all, one of them intended as a storehouse, one as a community kitchen and dining room, and the others each containing five small bedrooms, a bath, and a minute sitting room. The walls, after being opened at full length, fitted precisely into their neighbors by means of grooves and iron clasps. For underpinning, steel rods were forced into the frozen soil at seven-foot intervals to a depth of several feet; while, for added protection, the dwellings were erected against a bluff that would shut out the north wind, though there was no way of excluding the blasts from the sea, which beat against gray cliffs thirty feet below.

Another advantage of our location was that fresh water could be obtained from the little stream that rippled at one side and fell with a hoarse roar into the ocean. Artistically, no doubt, not much was to be said for our twenty-eight-foot square dwellings, with their roofs that rose to a uniform steep angle so as to throw off the snow, their unadorned dark brown sides, their storm windows made purposely narrow to retain maximum heat, their kerosene lamps and oil stoves for use until electricity was installed, and their spare, unadorned interiors. All in all, however, we were delighted.

Our first night on Icy Isle—or, rather, our first sleep, since the sun at that season did not set—was passed in these houses on cots from *The Comet*.

Before the vessel again took to the air, a group of us chanced to be standing near the cliff edge, watching the waves sullenly burst against the weathered rocks. Suddenly Norwood wheeled toward our leader.

"Listen here, Steve, I don't want to seem a Calamity Jane, but I can't get those damaged compartments out of my mind. Why not play safe, and have them repaired?"

"I've thought of that," Rathbone admitted. "Trouble is, to find proper repair facilities, we'd have to go as far as Vancouver, or maybe Seattle, and figure on a week or ten days' delay. You know what that would mean."

"Yes, I realize summer here is only a few weeks long, and is well advanced already. Just the same, I'd put first things first."

"But what *is* first? If the repairs aren't necessary, we'd be tying ourselves up all for nothing. What do you say, McDougal?"

"I'd say there was no need of it," testified the chief engineer, who had just ambled up.

"That's my view, too," volunteered Captain Knowlson. "An extra two or three-thousand-mile flight, Mr. Rathbone, isn't to be taken lightly."

And so the debate went on and on. From the first it was evident that Rathbone would not consent to the delay unless it seemed unavoidable. But although I was prepared for the verdict, a chill shot along my spine.

My companions, not sharing my fears, gave a rousing farewell when *The Comet,* with her crew of eight, rose proudly above the island and soared southward across the ice-infested sea, at first a huge cigar-shaped patch gliding through the serene clear air, then a mere dark speck against a remote cloud fringe, then less than a speck to the staring watchers.

And now for the most important task since our arrival! We had to know more about our surroundings; select a spot for our excavations "We'll explore, if possible, as far as the base of Devil's Peak," Rathbone decided, "and survey the country on an expedition lasting maybe eight or ten hours."

As half of us had to remain at camp, storing and making an inventory of *The Comet's* cargo, we cast lots to pick the explorers. Surely the gods were with me! The first to be chosen was Ada, and the fourth was myself; while Allenham was selected to remain in company with the packing cases.

At first our course lay over undulating tundra, carpeted with a green plush of lichens and moss. But after a mile or two, we began to ascend amid rugged masses of rock, on which the vegetation appeared only in scattered tufts. Even so, the slope was not precipitous, though in places it was irregular and broken. What particularly impressed me was the solitude, the emptiness; the cool, fresh air had a vitalizing effect; and as we pushed ahead I chatted gaily with Ada.

Now, when from time to time I glanced at our leader, I saw that the scientist in him was again uppermost: with painstaking care, he examined plants and rock strata, or scrutinized some particle of earth or stone. Once, in particular, when he was about a dozen paces ahead, I stopped short at his resounding cry. "By heaven! What do you make of this?"

He was speaking to the young geologist, James Kenworthy. In one hand he displayed a reddish brown rocky mass.

Kenworthy mumbled something that I could not make out; took the reddish mass; examined it with signs of interest; then passed it back with the remark, "No, there can't be any doubt."

"Well, Steve," I asked, pressing forward, "what's your great discovery?"

He thrust the red rock beneath my nose. "See this, Rod?"

"Looks like an iron oxide," I said, as I turned the rock slowly over in my hands.

"So it is—but it's more than that. Kenworthy was just pointing out its peculiar texture, which leads us to believe it's the combustion product of molten or vaporized iron hurled up during an eruption."

"Goodness gracious!" exclaimed Ada. "Then you think this island is volcanic?"

"I don't think it; I know it," Steve rumbled, pointing to a satiny, shining rock that in places seemed almost translucent. "Just look at that glassy structure. And that rough, rolling surface, rising in irregular bends and ridges. There's only one explanation, isn't there, Kenworthy?"

"Afraid so," nodded the geologist. "The rocks hereabouts are predominantly basaltic. We're now walking over cooled lava."

"What's more," added Rathbone, "it couldn't have cooled very long ago. Everywhere, you'll observe, it occurs in the surface layers. The absence of any overlying deposits suggests no great lapse of geologic time."

"You mean," I gasped, "there's been an eruption in recent years?"

"Well, comparatively recent," corrected Kenworthy. "A few hundred years, maybe a few thousand. On an island like this, it's hard to estimate the time, since there wouldn't be any great wind-blown deposits, or any large amount of organic remains to cover up the lava. On the other hand, there's no evidence of submersion beneath the sea, which would be probable with the passage of many geologic ages."

"So we're near a live volcano right now?" asked Ada, her vivid blue eyes agleam. "If there's been one eruption, maybe they'll be another?"

"Not at all likely, at least for a time yet. Eruptions usually occur only at wide intervals, and haven't ever been reported in these latitudes at all."

"So Devil's Peak is the volcano?"

"You can take my word it is. Notice its peculiar shape—how split and broken it is. That opening there" —he pointed to the mouth of the great face roughly outlined by the peak—"was clearly caused by the explosive escape of lava through some fissure. And that flat patch—that wide level space at the summit—is almost certainly where you'd find the main crater, if you climbed high enough."

"Well, this *is* news," I admitted. "But after all, can it really matter much whether or not we're on a volcanic isle?"

Rathbone's heavy features contracted in a frown.

"Don't be too sure, Rod! When we get to boring, we may find the temperature greatly affected by the hidden volcanic energy."

Ada and I were about to add some questions, when a cry from ahead of us snapped the discussion short. Norwood, a hundred yards in the vanguard, was motioning wildly; and as we rushed up to him through a defile of ridged and twisted rock, we came upon a scene of magic.

Here was the lake which he had mentioned. Deeply blue, with the bewitching tint of glacial water, it stretched for miles along the folds of snowy hills, its surface varied by the white of drifting ice floes and miniature bergs, its entire western shore flanked by the slopes of a great glacier. Across from us, three or four miles away, Devil's Peak lifted its frozen heights amid a black-and-white confusion of foothills.

"It's just as if some enchantress ruled with a story-book charm," remarked Ada. "And yet there's something unfriendly about it. It's so frosty my teeth want to chatter!"

From that comment the waters took their name. "Frost Lake," they were ever afterwards called.

VI

Rathbone now had no trouble laying his plans.

"See that meadow between those low ridges," he explained, as we stood together on a rocky crest, "That's where our excavations begin. It's not more than about half a mile from camp. We'll connect a series of large pipes from the lake to the meadow, and build an electric powerplant at the ocean edge a few hundred yards from the shaft."

"But won't we need some sort of road between the powerplant and tunnel, and between both spots and the settlement?"

Steve broke into a low, short laugh.

"Don't think I've overlooked that, do you, Rod? No, I'm planning an electrically lighted road to run as close as possible to the shelter of the rock embankment down there, with automatic snow-sweeping equipment."

Within a day or two, with the aid of jeeps and a light bulldozer, we were constructing the road and the powerhouse. The latter, prefabricated like our dwellings, was thrown up in a few hours—a long one-story building, with several wings, each surmounted by a sharply peaked roof. I was not surprised to see the dynamos, which had been taken from *The Comet,* and which the dog teams had a hard time hauling to the powerhouse when the road was ready; but I was amazed at the profusion of long hollow steel rods. Each was several inches thick; each was capable of fitting into others like it, while many were featured by immense springs attached to one end.

"Just another of my inventions, Rod," confided Rathbone, smiling enigmatically. "Didn't I tell you of my scheme to generate electricity from the ice pressure?"

"I believe you did mention it."

"Well, maybe I pointed out, ice power is one of the world's great sources of unutilized energy. Remember this, Rod: the ice fields are hundreds of miles wide and average three to twelve feet in thickness, though in places they're twenty, fifty, yes, even a hundred and twenty feet deep. The pressure ridges, which are often fifty or sixty feet high and miles long, are thrown up by the thousands every winter."

"You mean, they're caused by the ice pressure?"

"By that, and nothing else. So I propose to tap this unused force."

"Sounds good. But is it as easy as all that?"

"It's not too hard. Often, even during the extreme cold, the pack will split, leaving lanes of open water, or 'leads,' which come together with shattering force. I intend, among other things, to take advantage of these openings. The end of my steel tubes will be crossed at right angles by stout metal disks yards across, so that, when the tubes are joined together and stretch far out across the ice, the surface of the disks may rest against the further side of a lead. When the lead closes, my apparatus will be pushed back with tremendous power—"

"Yes, and snapped!"

"They might be, except for the springs. But these are the crux of the invention. They're each several feet thick, as maybe you've noticed; and they contract to absorb a pressure of many tons to the square inch. The colossal energy transmitted by them to the rods will be transmitted in turn to another series of springs, and then, by means of wheels and revolving chains, will be conveyed to the dynamos, which will convert it into electricity very much according to the principles we use in water-power generators."

"Seems ingenious," I acknowledged. "But won't it be risky to depend too much upon the leads?"

"I'm not depending on them too much. I'll have several machines, some relying on the pressure of the pack against the shore."

"And will that give power enough?"

"Enough?" From under his bushy brows, Rathbone shot me a gleam of amusement. "Ten times more than enough! Why, it'll light and heat our houses; do most of our chores; and give us current for an electric pumping plant, which we'll need in excavating by a new plan."

"Why should you need a pumping plant in excavating?"

But before Rathbone could reply, foreman "Sandy" Scruggs approached with a blueprint and a question about the powerhouse.

Our first three days on Icy Isle had given us no hint of the hidden weather demons. But the fourth day brought a change. Our spirits were chilled by one of those fogs that were frequent guests on Icy Isle;

and the fog was followed by a drizzling rain, succeeded by a gale.

By this time, we were worried about *The Comet,* which was expected back next day from Nome. Rathbone, of course, assured us that she was weather-proof; but as a twilight gloom settled over the world and we sat in our kerosene-lighted houses, heating ourselves by the ill-smelling oil stoves, we passed many an anxious hour.

Next day, however, the wind quieted, the clouds lifted and the sun reappeared. And now we all thronged the beach, several of us with binoculars, eagerly searching the air. And promptly at the scheduled hour, a shout went up—low down amid the remote blue, a minute black object, little more than a wavering speck, gradually expanded into a silvery ellipse, then into a huge gliding fish-shaped vessel.

Captain Knowlson, after an uneventful trip, declared that the damaged compartments had caused no trouble. And oh, the false sense of security this gave us! During the next few weeks, *The Comet* made six round trips to Nome, returning each time with provisions, pipes, tools and machinery delivered by steamer to the Alaskan port. Before she set out on her seventh and last scheduled trip, even the gloomiest of us had

come to think of the run from Nome to Icy Isle almost
as of an excursion from New York to Jersey City.

By this time we had been on the island more than
a month, and knew that winter was around the corner.
Nevertheless, the weather was still not severe. Even
on the second and third days after *The Comet's* departure, when a gale blustered out of the north, we
were not uneasy; and on the fourth day, when *The
Comet* was due to return, most of us were still undis-
turbed, and many of us were not sufficiently concerned
to join the watchers on the beach to welcome the
ship's reappearance.

Nevertheless, the day was a wild and frightening
one. Great ragged clouds drifted crazily across heavens
by turns sunny and obscured, while the screeching of
the wind merged with the thundering of the waves and
the occasional crunching and grinding of great ice cakes
slapped and pounded together.

Norwood and most of my comrades on the beach
shivered a little, and strode back and forth to keep
warm while rubbing their hands together vigorously.
Yet they all seemed without premonitions. All, that is,
except Allenham. Having left shelter partly because
he would have been bored to distraction indoors, but
chiefly because Ada had coaxed him out, he was in no

cheerful mood.

"You know, I keep wondering if that pesky ship will ever get back," I overheard him saying during a break in the wind, as he pulled a well-shaped hat down over his ears and drew his camel's hair coat tightly about his shoulders. "It's strange, but I just feel something in my marrow."

"Why, Alan, how can you say such a thing?" Ada threw at him reproachfully. As I stepped up, she turned to me in almost tearful appeal. "Everything's as safe as our own doorstep, isn't it, Rodney? *The Comet* can't be in danger!"

"Not in the least!" I lied, and was rewarded by a grateful smile.

"Well, there's nothing like going to an authority," scoffed Allenham, in that affected drawl that made me want to knock him down.

But a sudden gust choked my retort. And when I had regained my breath I could see Allenham's back, as head down, he went scuttling off toward the settlement.

An hour more, and still no sign of the dirigible. Two hours, three hours, while watches were consulted frequently and few spoke. Rathbone, a solitary figure pacing the beach with a grim-set face, refused to answer questions. "Wait, and we'll see!" he would snap. Or, taking his eyes from the storm-troubled sea and sky, he would mutter, as if to himself, "In a head wind like this, what can you expect? Their speed will be held down. Another hour or two, and they'll be here."

But I could not help noticing the haggard features, the bloodshot eyes, the pallid cheeks.

Frequently, as if to test our patience, the wind would die down, only to spring up again with redoubled energy. And as it screamed across the white-caps and over the groaning ice blocks, I could have imagined that I heard the shriek of a demon's derision.

At last almost every member of our small colony was on the beach, most of us shivering, most of us fighting the greater chill in our hearts.

Then, when the tension seemed near the snapping point, the long-awaited word was heard. Norwood, who with binoculars had been balking the wind on a little ridge of rock, startled us all with a great shout.

"There she comes!"

In a yelling mob, we flocked about him, almost crowding him off his eminence. One by one we took brief looks through the binoculars. And fervent exclamations came to our lips.

After a few minutes, even the naked eye could make out the object speeding toward us not far above the wavecrests.

But our cries of thanksgiving died even as we uttered them. When the dirigible was almost over the island's nearer tip, suddenly we noticed something peculiar about her movements. Instead of advancing with her usual steady glide, she began to describe queer loops and zigzags. She lunged from side to side, sagged in her stern or dipped as for a nose dive; then, after righting herself and sailing for a moment on an even course, she would repeat the whole performance, diving and twisting and soaring anew.

Gradually, however, she did draw nearer, her cigar-shaped frame looming large between us and the ragged accumulating clouds. For one instant, a dazzling delusive instant, hope rushed back over us, only to be quenched like a wave-drowned candle. Was a madman at *The Comet's* helm? All at once her movements became more fantastic, more uncontrolled than ever. Her stern, slanting almost straight downward, sent the white spray flying; then the whole craft shot skyward, then down once more with the violence of a bucking bronco.

The clouds, draping the sun with thick wreaths, had dulled everything to a sullen half-light which was neither night nor day. By this ghastly illumination, the spectacle was like something out of a nightmare: the blank curving beach, the dark rollers scattering foam, the huddled figures: Rathbone, clenching his fists till the nails bit into the flesh; Ada, her lips drawn apart in silent prayer; Norwood, aloof on his ridge, staring with steady gaze across the waste; some of the men swaying to and fro in restless torment, or standing still and crossing themselves.

The most unbearable part of it all, I think, was that we had to wait there, inert, helpless, as the vessel staggered on and on. Sometimes, in the uncertain light, we thought we could make out little black forms dashing about the heaving deck. But miracle followed miracle as, time after time, the ship escaped the depths that opened to receive her; time after time, though her sides were gray from the splashing salt water, she lifted herself again on her drunken flight. And at last she seemed about to descend upon the cliff-lined coast half a mile to our west.

Had she been able to hold out a few seconds longer, perhaps—yes, perhaps she would have escaped. Hope flamed up within us as we raced westward along the sands, struggling to get our breath against the furious wind-puffs; while the vessel, reaching a projecting fringe of the cliffs, shuddered like some harassed living thing, and hovered high in air as if seeking a suitable landing.

But she hovered for only a second. Her stern dipped earthward. Down, down! abruptly she fell. An instant before the nasty nerve-rending din smashed upon our ears, we saw the great form submerged in an eruption of foam at the cliff's base.

A few seconds later, a distorted mass of metal lay half visible amid the frothy waves and the ice floes.

And the wind, leaping up more uproariously than ever, seemed to shout in mockery and exultation.

VII

In a long straggling line, each pushing ahead as fast as the shrieking gusts would permit, we made our way along the beach and around the cliffs, where we could see the great metal hulk of *The Comet,* her stern impaled on an outlying reef and ripped into two huge, half-severed segments. We were still too stunned to grasp the full import of the disaster; but as we raced along the wet sands, one question kept repeating itself. What had happened to the men?

Hardly realizing that I risked death, I waded at times knee-deep through the icy surges, at other times sought my balance on some slippery ledge. As I gazed across the white-sprayed shoals to the seemingly inaccessible dirigible, I was spurred on by the sight of one who, by accident, was racing at my side: a tall, athletic girl, her face tense with terror and her bobbed hair flying loose, while she kept on with a determination that challenged my utmost exertion.

For all our speed, some of the men had preceded us, sometimes seeking the treacherous foothold of an ice cake, sometimes slipping into the chill waters. None, apparently, had eyes except for that great shapeless mass of metal which, as we drew nearer, showed seams and gashes where compartment after compartment had been wrenched open.

As I rounded a turn of the cliffs and came in full sight of the wreck, I stopped short with a gasp. Ada, at my side, turned to me with stricken eyes. What we saw was a vast foam-beaten hulk, lying like some ghostly behemoth in the gray twilight beneath the low scudding clouds. Though parts almost touched the shore, other portions lay deep in the waves. The cabins were under water!

Ada's lips opened in a muffled cry as she pointed to the deck promenade—the space between roof and water level was hardly more than two feet! Even if the men had survived the fall, surely they had all drowned!

"Wait here!" I shouted to Ada, and could not tell whether she had heard me when, balancing on a half-submerged reef, I started toward the vessel. My eyes were on her forward section, which contained the cabins; and it was more luck than skill that enabled me to reach the ship's side, where I clung to the battered metal projections and pressed onward by slow, hazardous steps.

As I drew near the cabins, was I raving mad to think I heard a sound which was not that of winds or waters? I stood stock-still, listening; and after a moment, the sound was repeated. Long-drawn and dismal, it seemed hardly human; seemed like the moan of a beast in pain. But following it immediately there came another sound, sharper and more distinct. "Help! Help! Help!"

"Where are you?" I called back, my heart galloping. "Where are you?"

Several forms, during the ensuing brief interval, came scurrying toward me across the rocks.

"Where are you?" I yelled once more. But there was no reply.

By this time the dark forms, splashing, wading, half-swimming, had come near enough for me to recognize Norwood's grim, determined face, followed by the specter-white Rathbone and then by McPherson, one of the workmen.

"Don't you see?" Steve bawled into my ears, as he grasped my arm furiously. "They're still there! In the cabins!"

The wind, rising again in a convulsive volley, answered him like a sneer. The breakers leapt fiercely against the airship's torn sides, which seemed to be sinking by inches even as we watched.

Norwood, taking no time to explain, was already hastening toward the vessel's stern; waded thigh-deep; and plunged into a broken compartment near the storerooms.

A few seconds later he emerged, dripping and with ripped sleeves, but triumphantly waving two axes. Instantly, being a little in advance of the others, I seized one of the implements.

Motioning me to follow, he climbed a ridge of rock that projected above the cabins, then recklessly crossed to the cabin roof and began to pound it with the axe. As I scrambled to his side and began hammering at the thin metal partition, every stroke seemed to shriek in our ears. "Hurry! Hurry! Hurry!"

From within the ship, all sounds may have ceased; amid the commotion of our blows, we could not have heard a foghorn. Perched perilously on the roof, beaten by the wind, each stroke threatening to throw us off, we banged and battered away, until the metal began to rip and we had knocked out a space several feet square.

Then what a sight from inside! The water came to within a foot or two of the cabin roof; but on the black surface, at the further end, a queer object floated. Only by straining our eyes could we recognize it as a wooden cot. And only after further straining did we identify a dim bobbing patch, and two long dark strips clinging to the cot.

While I cried out, reeled, and almost lost my balance, Norwood flung off his boots; then, so rapidly that I hardly realized what he intended, he had climbed through the ragged opening into the ice-cold water, swum to the floating cot, vanished for a second and reappeared, dragging a dark, trailing form. As I dove after him, I recognized the deathly face and closed eyes of chief engineer McDougal.

It required all Norwood's mighty energy, and all my own waning strength, to life the lifeless form out of the wrecked compartment and down to the refuge of the rocks. Yet, as soon as the stricken man had been extricated and left in the care of Dr. Straub, who worked over him avidly, Norwood and I hurled ourselves again into the ship's icy heart, where the captain and six of the crew remained unaccounted for.

By this time, Rathbone, McPherson and half a dozen others had joined us. Looking back upon the risks we took, I hold it miraculous that we escaped drowning in that sunken ship. Nowhere, as we forced our way from cabin to cabin, did we have more than two feet of leeway. Yet, with a despairing fury, we persisted. Here we would find a man clinging to an overturned table; there one that, nearly exhausted, had made a haven of a drifting mattress. Half-conscious men, bruised, gashed, and with broken ribs, were buoyed up on chairs, boxes and slabs of ice. But finally the last victim had been rescued; then, panting and shivering, we struggled back to the ledges, where our comrades supported our collapsing forms and led us to a great bonfire in a sheltered corner of the cliffs.

But it was not our physical injuries that concerned us as we lay close to the vitalizing flames, listening to the screech of the wind and the waves and ice blocks that pounded the shore. Over us all there had fallen a dread realization. Our one means of communication with the world had been shattered. We were marooned on Icy Isle!

VIII

Blankness . . . blankness . . . blankness . . . long intervals of unconsciousness, varied by half-conscious stretches, when a throbbing in the head and a pain in the chest made it difficult to move. By turns I was chilled and burning; troubled by delirious fancies.

At first I could not understand what these distorted visions meant. But after a time I grasped the truth. I had suffered a congestion of the lungs. For many weeks —six or eight—I lay upon my cot, sometimes rallying, more than once close to the last borderline. I was vaguely aware now and then of hasty comings and goings, excited scurryings; and from time to time I recognized faces: the grave, worn features of Dr. Straub; the severe faces of Rathbone and Norwood, radiating sympathy and concern.

Then by degrees my impressions became sharper.

One day, after a refreshing sleep, I noticed for the first time the appearance of my sickroom; the plain dull brown walls; the glass of water and medicines on the tiny table beside my cot; the gray light filtering in through the curtained rectangle of the window. But these were not what held my attention. Bending above me were two trembling lips, two great blue solicitous eyes.

"Ada!" I exclaimed, recognizing her with a start of joy. And as I drew my hand from beneath the coverlet, seeking to take hers, I saw how the blue veins stood out on my wasted wrist.

"Don't speak!" she cautioned, putting her fingers to her lips and smiling wanly. "You musn't exert."

But from that moment, I knew that I would get well.

I could hardly help getting well, in view of her visits. She came every day, and sometimes would sit knitting at my bedside, forbidding me to speak, her head tilted to the left in her peculiar winsome way, while her smile was all the radiance I needed.

Then one day, when the returning strength of convalescence made life once more seem worth-while, Ada thought me well enough to hear some dismal news. "At first, you know, Rodney, we couldn't give you all the attention you needed. Too many of us were sick all at once."

"What's that?" I demanded, startled.

"We didn't want to tell you before," she went on, while I noticed the delicate shadings of those tender eyes, which in the varying light took on a violet tint that was elfin and mysterious. "But now, Rodney, I think you can bear to know. Captain Knowlson and the rescued men were—oh, so desperately sick all at the same time. Also, three of the rescuers beside yourself. Everything considered, we're lucky we could save so many."

"So many?" I gasped, sitting up in bed, while a sudden pain gripped my chest. "Then we didn't save everybody?"

Ada shook her head sadly. The lovely eyes seemed clouded with an almost purple opaqueness. "We got everyone out of the wreck, of course. But Philip Andrews—you knew him, a big husky laughing crewman—he didn't last out the day. And Peter McFane—the bustling little man with the russet-apple cheeks—died a few days later of pneumonia."

"Poor devils!" I groaned.

"Some of the others are still in bed," Ada went on, her eyes brightening again to violet. "But, thank goodness, they're all getting better."

She sighed wearily, and for the first time I noticed the worn cheeks, which had exchanged their rose complexion for a gray-white pallor.

"Ada," I blurted out, "you've been working too hard taking care of us—taking care of me—"

"Oh, don't flatter yourself!" she cut me short, while a faint red crossed her face and ran down the slim neck. "I wasn't doing any more for you than for anyone. Being the only white woman in camp, naturally I had to volunteer as nurse. That's all there is to it."

Somehow, I knew that there was not all there was to it.

After that, my recovery was rapid. "Take it easy, young man, don't walk too fast or far, and maybe you'll give me a rest for a while," counselled Dr. Straub in granting me permission to go outside again. And Ada volunteered to be my guide and escort!

Taking my arm—strictly, she insisted, in her capacity as nurse—she led me slowly out of doors. But she smiled at me in her old whimsical gay manner.

A change had come over the world. Although it was but two in the afternoon, the stars glittered with a metallic brilliance from the frosty skies; and the North Star was almost directly overhead. At the same time, a ghostly spectacle flickered above: thin, unreal, ghostly streamers, which wavered across the sky in spectral wreaths and curtains, impalpable, intangible, the culminating touch of fantasy.

But even as I stared at the witch-fire of the aurora, a booming as of a remote explosion, shocked me out of my mood of awe. Instantly another followed, sharp, prolonged and grinding, reminding me of the ripping and wrenching of great steel masses.

"Lord, what is it?" I exclaimed, with horrifying visions of Rathbone's power plant blown to dust.

Ada's amusement was evident.

"Only the ice," she explained. "The weather's been warmer these last few days; the ice is breaking up. With your windows all closed, you couldn't hear the racket, the houses being soundproof."

As Ada and I kept on across the starlit tundra, with the wind howling in gusts, I saw all about me a mixture of the civilized and primitive. Strung above us against a low bluff, the electric lights showed us the way; but, like a flashback to an earlier age, a dog team came crawling toward us, seven beasts straining in harness to pull the heavily laden sledge, with the driver striding behind, lash in hand.

"Well, I'll be blasted! What you doing here, John?"

I burst out, seeing Norwood in this unexpected rôle.

"Oh, just a little animal training. Keeps a fellow fit," he answered, laughing. And with a grin and a flick of the whip, he had passed on.

"But is this really necessary?"

"Yes," Ada answered. "The jeeps and other motorized equipment—there just aren't enough to go round. Besides, now that *The Comet's* lost, we'll have to be careful about fuel."

Within a few minutes we had come into sight of the snow-covered projection of the powerhouse. Extending from that building along the icy sea, a series of metal tubes and rods were barely visible for a few hundred yards by the dim artificial illumination, then vanished into the shadows of the ice pack. These, I knew, were the electric generators.

"Maybe we'll find Steve in the powerhouse," Ada conjectured. "However, he's just about as often in the pit."

"What pit?"

"You haven't heard? That's the name we've given the main tunnel—the one that will make Ice Isle green and fruitful."

Ada had spoken with the old assurance; but somehow, as I gazed at the bleak, dim waste of wintry sea and land, I could not visualize leafy fields, golden harvests, rose-trellised cottages, arbors and orchards.

As we entered the building, an oily smell attacked our nostrils; the whirring and rumbling of machines crashed upon our ears. I caught a glimpse of dynamos in a long line, amid labyrinths of wheels, wires, rotating chains and fast-moving levers. But Ada, not pausing, led me toward a door placarded in red: "S. RATHBONE. OFFICE."

We were just about to knock when a crimson-faced man shot out, his lips twisted in a nasty curl.

"Oh, you, Alan!"

Allenham paused just long enough to sweep us with a glance, mumbled something hoarse-sounding, then with a scowl strode down the hall and out of the building, slamming the door behind him.

"Gracious! What's getting into him?" Ada mumbled, a flush crossing her face as we slipped into the office.

Seated with a smile at a pine desk was the head and master of the expedition.

"Ada! And Rod!" he greeted us, springing up and squeezing my hand in a hearty grip. "Well! You're looking your old self again! You know, Rod, there were moments when I didn't expect ever to see you here."

As I clasped my old friend's hand and stared him full in the face, I noticed the difference in him. It was not only that grizzled strands were appearing at the base of his long, badly cropped hair; it was not that his big square jaw seemed to close with a more steely decisiveness than ever. There was something more intangible: visible in the lines that in certain moods ran down from the corners of his lips; visible, also, in an iron quality of the deep-sunken gray eyes.

The room's very appearance, I thought, was significant. All about the desk, whose three drawers had been pulled out to various distances, the papers lay scattered in confusion. Some of them, I saw, were crowded with scribbled notes, some were filled with figures and chemical formulae; and these documents were interspersed with a wilderness of notebooks and mechanical drawings and charts. To Rathbone's left an open typewriter stood, and to his right a telephone.

After we had stripped off our fur coats and taken seats, several enthusiastic minutes passed while I commended the progress of our project. Ada, shifting uneasily in her chair, seemed not to hear anything we said.

"We passed Alan just now at the door," she finally threw out, during a pause in the discussion.

Rathbone popped forward in his seat as if snapped by a spring.

"Yes? Found him in a sociable mood, did you?"

We both remained silent.

"I'm sorry to mention it, Ada," Rathbone continued, after a long pause, "but you might as well know. Alan and I—well, we've come to a little understanding."

"Understanding?"

"I hadn't meant to trouble you about these things, Ada dear. I might as well let you in on the facts before you get somebody's distorted version. You, too, Rod," he urged, as I rose to leave. "The situation is simply stated. Alan's been a slacker."

"Slacker? No, you don't mean it, Steve!"

"It's God's truth. He's had the benefit of every doubt."

Rathbone's bull-like face shot resolutely forward. With a grim smile, he turned to me.

"You see, Rod, it's this way. We're engaged in a desperate gamble, everybody must do his share. I've assigned every last man of us a task, which I expect him to perform—out of a sense of honor, if he has one. But as the head of this expedition, I have to use my authority for the sake of us all. That's where the sparks began to fly between me and Alan. He's the hardest man

in camp to fit into place. He can't do either scientific
work or hard manual labor. I've given much thought
to the matter, as you know, Ada, before finding the
one job I supposed he could fill. As elevator man for
the pit, he would be warm, and not overworked. But
did he try to make good? For a few days he did work
half-heartedly, then quit without even giving notice.
So I summoned him here this afternoon and laid down
the law."

"What law, Steve?" asked Ada, looking pale and distressed.

Rathbone's jaw came together with the firmness of
a trap snapping. One clenched fist pounded the desk,
sending half a dozen papers fluttering to the floor.

"The law's very simple. He who will not work
shall not eat! That's all there is to it, and nothing
could be fairer. Since no provisions can be handed out
without my order, Alan won't have another meal till
he does something to deserve it."

A big tear rolled unchecked across Ada's left cheek.

"But to try to starve him into submission, Steve—oh,
that's cruel! What if he went on a hunger strike?"

"What! Alan?" Rathbone almost shouted wth laughter. "No, don't you worry, Ada. He's used to a well-
filled stomach."

With an unsentimental decisiveness he thrust his chair back, and turned to me again.

"Maybe you'll be surprised, Rod, to see me such a despotic brute. But what would you do with seventy-three human lives in your keeping, as well as a project that may save this struggling planet for another five hundred generations? Wouldn't you know that any rebellion, if you allowed it to seep in, would grow like a weed?"

"I believe you're right, Steve."

"I know I'm right!" he insisted, with characteristic positiveness. And then, with a swift change of mood, he leapt up and placed a consoling hand on Ada's shoulder. "Don't take it too hard, Sis. We're not going to do anything drastic to Alan. A little discipline, he'll get over his anger, and it'll be all for his good."

Then, swinging back to me, "Well, Rod, guess you'd like to see just what we've been doing while you were sick? We haven't exactly wasted our time. Suppose we step over for a look at the pit?"

"Nothing I'd like better!" I assented, as Rathbone reached for his fur coat.

IX

For a few hundred yards we trudged through the hard
firm snow along an electrically lighted roadway. Then,
after mounting a little rise in the land, we saw an
enormous funnel-shaped mass in an artificially illumi-
nated space just ahead: a metallic projection possibly
fifty feet high, twenty feet across at the base and forty
feet wide at the summit. Four or five little huts, with
pipes and wires piled in disorder on all sides, were
scattered beneath the main structure; and several fur-
encased men were working in the yellowish artificial
glow, which every few seconds was varied by a whitish
glare when the door of one of the huts swung open,
revealing a blazing interior where huge wheels rotated.

At first it did not occur to me that this was "the pit."
But Rathbone enlightened me.

"There is one of the vents for waste products," he

explained. And he pointed to a little ditch, marked, "POISON: KEEP AWAY!" where a greenish-yellow oily-looking liquid was flowing seaward from an opening in the great funnel.

When we reached the huts, several men paused to nod to Rathbone deferentially. I could see in each a little of the distant respect of a military subordinate to his officer.

Pushing between Ada and me and taking us each by the arm, Rathbone led us into the largest hut and down a stairway to a well-lighted underground room.

"Elevator'll be here in just a minute," he stated, as he pressed a push-button. "The shaft, a separate tube—as in the model you saw—already goes nearly to the pit bottom. We've installed one of the fastest elevators made. While Alan was playing hooky, I've had to appoint Bill Hendrickson, thought he could be more valuable in other ways."

Rathbone had hardly finished when we heard a clattering and the elevator door opened with a bang. But it was not Hendrickson that stood before us.

With a whipped-dog look, Allenham averted his eyes. I noticed the baleful flash beneath his down-slanting lids.

"All the way down!" Rathbone directed. And the

door slammed behind us; with a needlessly severe jerk
we were launched into the descent.

As the door swung open below, Ada turned to Steve
and me with a smile, "You boys excuse me, won't you?
See you when you come back."

I nodded a none too eager assent. But I did my best
to forget my jealousy as Rathbone introduced me to
the pit. It was as he had said—he had not exactly wasted
his time. After following him through a low, narrow
gallery, I came out upon a little wooden balcony that
projected into a tunnel of imposing size about twenty-
five feet across, cut perpendicularly through the solid
rock into the indeterminate depths. Above us, the stars
glittered through the black circle of the opening.

"We're now at the three-hundred-yard level," Rathbone reported. "We've cut down already to three hundred and forty-two yards. Maybe you'd like a clearer
view."

Pressing a button, he flooded the lower reaches of
the pit with light. Now I could see pipes as thick as my
arm clamped to the rock wall; wires and rope ladders
all along the sides of the excavation, reaching from
wooden balcony to balcony; a large electric pump
standing on the lower balcony a hundred feet beneath;
and still farther down, at the base of the pit, a greenish-

yellow oily-looking viscid liquid.

"Lord, Steve!" I enthused. "You must be going in for a world's tunnel-drilling speed record! How in—"

He cut me short with a hasty wave of the hand.

"That's one of my little surprises, Rod. Fact is that I've installed a new system of excavating. Hasn't the inadequacy of the old methods ever occurred to you?"

"Can't say I've given it much thought."

"Even the most advanced means—bulldozers, steam dredges, pneumatic rock drills, dynamite—are so slow it would take us years to bore far enough down, though we do need some dynamite for minor blasting. Naturally, we must have a quicker method. Can't you guess what?"

"Not atomic power?"

"Of course not! That would be too much for us to handle. But maybe I can explain it all in a phrase. I've discovered a universal solvent."

"What? A substance that dissolves all other substances? But such a thing has never been known!"

"No," Rathbone agreed, smiling. "Neither was radium known before Madame Curie."

"You mean to say, Steve, your substance is as remarkable as radium?"

"That sounds like an excessive claim," he conceded;

and the smile had not left his face. "Yet it's exactly what I mean. Tri-nitro-fluoric acid is the most powerful non-fissionable chemical reagent ever obtained. Not that it has the explosive qualities of certain nitrogen compounds—"

"Or of the atom or hydrogen bomb?"

"No. But it has some equally valuable properties, the chief of which is its extraordinary chemical activity. Maybe there are some substances, Rod, which it won't combine with, but I haven't found any yet, aside from the inert gases. Strangely, the product of the union, in almost every case, is a thick, oily liquid such as you see down there at the bottom of the pit."

In a stunned sort of way, I went on to ask how he had discovered the acid.

"Well, I can't take much credit," he admitted with a deprecatory shrug. "Maybe you know I'd been experimenting for years to find a more powerful solvent. At last, after I'd worked till I was bleary-eyed, I discovered a new fluorine compound—one of the most corrosive acids ever generated, as I can testfy from the sores that broke out on my hands and face from contact with its vapors. There wasn't any common metal that it wouldn't dissolve and many non-metals, too, would melt away before it. I hardly know what it was one day that gave me the idea of mixing it with a semi- explosive nitrogen compound I'd just originated. Looking back, I'd say it was a crazy thing; I risked being blown to atoms. But luck was with me. As soon as I'd poured the two substances together, I noticed a furious bubbling and a peculiar sour smell; then a clear yellow liquid formed in the glass container."

"If it was a universal solvent," I objected, "it would consume the glass."

"What makes you think it didn't? Why, in less time than it took me to gasp, the bottle had melted away. All that was left was viscid fluid, which gnawed through the zinc lining of the laboratory table, then through the wood, then on into the concrete floor. Just try to picture my surprise! Here was a chemical that dissolved one of the most stable substances on earth!"

"Maybe so," I argued, "but glass is also attacked by another fluorine compound, hydrofluoric acid—"

"In that case, however," Rathbone broke in impatiently, "the action isn't nearly so rapid. I saw that I had something epoch-making. I was frantic to put it to the test, and made other experiments with fanatic speed. Well, I've already told you the results."

"But you haven't told me all, if this acid dissolves everything, how do you find a container for it?"

Rathbone grinned.

"A very good point. But who said I'd found any container? The truth is we probably never will find one. That does make it hard to analyze the compound, but doesn't affect it's actual uses. Tri-nitro-fluoric acid is my chief excavator."

"The mystery deepens."

"But there isn't any mystery. Before coming to Icy Isle, I manufactured large quantities of both components of the acid, and, thank heaven! brought them here before *The Comet* went down. From time to time we pour small amounts of both substances into the center of the funnel above the pit, of course keeping them clear of the walls. The acid forms instantly and dissolves all the earth and rock which it touches; as it always eats directly down, I can control it exactly. The sour-smelling resulting gases are light enough to pass out through the funnel. The poisonous liquid residue, which I call Trinitrin, meanwhile is forced to the surface by a system of pipes and electric pumps, and drained into the sea, as you observed."

"Even so, you'll need prodigious amounts of the acid."

"Less than you'd think. Five pounds can liquefy a ton of rock. Our present supply, for this reason, is enough for the time being; and I can renew it by means of certain materials, which are as plentiful here as in most places."

I had opened my mouth for another question. But we were interrupted by a voice from the black recesses above.

"Hey, Mr. Rathbone! Mr. Rathbone!"

Rathbone made a funnel of his hands. "What is it?"

"Can you come up here? Gallery C, near Balcony 3. Make it right away!"

"Be with you in a jiffy!"

In tones meant to be calm, Rathbone remarked, "That's Kenworthy up there. He's always running into trouble. Excuse me, Rod. Elevator's right along that little gallery."

While I watched in astonishment, Rathbone stepped out upon the wooden platform, reached for one of the rope ladders, and, like a seaman climbing to the crow's nest of a ship, began to mount arm over arm, growing smaller and smaller until he had become but a dim shape far up among the shadows of the pit.

X

I pressed the elevator button. Minutes later, a sullen-looking Allenham stopped for me.

After a ride like that of deaf mutes, I was glad to step out again into the night. As I did so, a door burst open at the base of the funnel above the pit; and a man's head shot out, followed by a fur-clad body. And Rathbone, releasing himself from the rope ladder, stood grinning at my side; and in a moment was joined by the geologist, Kenworthy.

I was instantly struck by the two men's exultant looks and excited movements.

"Fine to see you here, Rod!" Rathbone panted. "I've got something to tell you! You'll be the first to learn of Kenworthy's discovery!"

"Not mine! Yours equally!" denied Kenworthy.

"Not at all! Yours in every way! But let's not

quarrel over honors. Here, Rod! Look at this!"

He tossed me what appeared to be a little black rock.

Comprehension came to me quickly enough. The little rock had a familiar charred appearance, and gave my hands a sooty smear.

"Coal!"

"You're tooting right, coal! Ever hear of such luck?" Rathbone enthused, striding back and forth in a paroxysm of glee. "Kenworthy struck a rich vein of it!"

I turned the little black pellet over and over in my hands. No pearls or diamonds could have had equal fascination.

"We'll start in mining right away!" Rathbone hastened on, once more the young enthusiast. "There'll be a thousand—no, ten thousand uses for the coal! We'll build furnaces to smelt iron ore—thank God that's also common here!"

"But how extensive is the vein?" I questioned, remembering that coal is a product of ancient vegetation. "It's hard to believe there's much of it in these latitudes—"

"That just shows how much you know!" Rathbone chided me impatiently. "Don't you realize, Rod, in distant geologic eras—millions of years ago—climatic conditions were different, and this region supported a lush life? Why, it's well known the poles have been shifting!"

"That's true, Mr. Farnsworth," Kenworthy contributed, "Coral—a tropical growth—has been observed on the coast of Greenland. A seam of coal ten feet thick has been mined in Spitzbergen—which, remember, is almost as far north as Icy Isle."

"Well, here's proof enough, isn't it?" Rathbone took up, dangling another bit of the black mineral before us. "The only question is precisely what to do with the coal."

"Well, with our electric generators in action," I contended, "we don't need it for heating—"

"Yes, but what about the summer, when the ice has broken up? Coal will be just the thing then to generate electricity."

"Meanwhile," added Kenworthy, "we can use it for fuel to forge rails and make cars for our electric railway between the settlement and the power plant and pit."

"Believe me, we will!" affirmed Rathbone. "We'll find more uses for it than the sea over there has ice drifts. The day may come when we'll thank our lucky stars for this discovery!"

XI

A few days later—or, rather, a few "sleeps"—Dr. Straub gave me my discharge, and said I might be assigned to regular duty. He recommended, however, that I spend much time outdoors, for my lungs showed the effects of my ailment.

And so one day I had an interview with Rathbone.

"Been wondering about you, Rod," he began, as he gravely drew one hand over his bristly square jaw. "I'm not sure just what you can do best. We'd originally thought, of course, of using you in your specialty. But the laboratory would be the worst thing for you, with a fine assortment of vile vapors to corrode your lungs. The powerhouse wouldn't be much better. And the same will be true of the coal mine, when we get to working it."

Thoughtfully he looked over a notebook crowded with his almost illegible scrawl.

"Naturally," he went on slowly, "I don't want to assign you some menial duty, such as helping the Eskimo women mend the garments, or officiating in the 'kitchen police.' However, I don't know just what else to suggest."

"Well, Steve, you know I'll willingly do anything at all."

A moment's silence followed, while Rathbone still studied his notebook with a pained look.

"Ah, here's something!" he suddenly discovered, with evident relief. But almost instantly the pleasure died from his expression. "No, I should know better."

"What is it?"

"Nothing you'd care about," he decided, closing the book. "Sorry to have brought it up, Rod."

"Why not let me judge for myself?"

He sat looking across at me severely.

"Well, no harm in mentioning it, I guess. You see, Rod, we could use another driver for the dog teams—one who could go hunting with the dogs. Our provisions are likely to run low before the winter's over; a little fresh meat would help out mightily. Just now, we have only three men that I'd trust with the dogs! Norwood, and the two Eskimo drivers. There are, as you know, fourteen dogs in all, and two men to a team wouldn't be too many—would be almost essential in corraling game far out on the ice and bringing it into camp."

Something within me took fire at this idea.

"What makes you think I couldn't qualify?"

"It's not that you couldn't qualify, Rod," he answered, scrutinizing me thoughtfully. "It's that the work wouldn't be your type. You haven't had the experience. Man, don't you realize the hazard of venturing out across the frozen sea? That ice is more treacherous than a rattlesnake; there's always the danger it may open and swallow you. Or the blizzards may blind and ambush you, with the cold at sixty below. Why, sometimes, even if you were only a hundred yards from home, you wouldn't be able to save yourself except by building a snow hut and camping there for days."

"Oh, so that's it?" I laughed. "I'm one of those mollycoddles who have to be wrapped in soft blankets? You surprise me, Steve! Since when have you sought the safe way yourself?"

"What I seek myself is beside the point, Rod. I've the right to risk my life. I haven't the right to risk yours."

"Good God, then you think there are no risks at camp? Listen, Steve! I'd very much like a try as dog driver and hunter. I may not have many qualifications, but I do have one. I've always had a way with dogs."

"Yes, but Eskimo dogs—they're quite another thing. They're only two jumps from the wolf. They look like wolves, act like wolves, fight like wolves; except for their curling tails, you might believe they were wolves."

"All the more reason I want to handle them."

Before the day was over, I had been launched into my new duties. And thus began my long partnership with Quinanquak (known for short as "Quin"), the younger Eskimo dog driver. Having gone to school at Nome, he spoke understandable English, and taught me how to feed the animals, how to control them, how to reward and punish them, how to prevent them from slashing at one another, how to hitch them up in a wide band, no two at the same distance from the sledge, how to detect shirkers and slackers and thwart their wiles and ruses. Sometimes Norwood would lend a timely word. And sometimes I would have the grunted advice of Norwood's Eskimo helper, Asukitsoq. And so, on the whole, I managed to get on. It was not many days before, having practiced for hours in flicking the long lash, I ventured out by myself with the team of seven "huskies," piloting them with a load of hundreds of pounds across the icy waste to the pit or power plant.

One day the tracks of a bear were seen near camp; and eager for food, I went off on its trail with "Quin." It led us astray much further than we realized, so that we were caught in one of the blizzards which sometimes sweep down on those parts with unbearable ferocity. Fortunately, Quin knew how to make a snow hut, and there we weathered out the storm, which Quin could withstand much better than I. When at last we struggled back to camp, I was exhausted, and once more lay for several days in bed, though my recovery was much more rapid than during my former illness.

It was only when I was nearly well again that I became aware that something was wrong in camp.

Suddenly I asked myself if Ada's strained expression, when at times she flitted into my sick room in her capacity as nurse, was due wholly to her fears for me. And I wondered if Rathbone looked so drawn and careworn simply because of my disappearance.

"Tell me, Steve, what's gone awry?" I asked Rathbone one day, when he came for a brief visit. "Don't say it's nothing—I can feel it like an electric charge in the air."

He stared at me with distressed level gray eyes.

"You're right," he acknowledged with characteristic

directness. "There's no reason now to keep it from you. Dr. Straub did insist we mustn't worry you about it. But it would worry you even more not to mention it."

"So what is it?" I gasped, sitting up in bed so suddenly that my heart gave a flutter. "No one's—no one's—"

My friend had sunk heavily into a seat at my side.

"No, no one's been killed. That, however, is largely a matter of luck. Several have been injured—fortunately, none fatally. Operations at the pit have been temporarily halted."

He sat staring at me with as melancholy an expression as I had ever seen on his face. For the first time in our long acquaintance, the great square head was bowed.

"What was it?" I demanded. "An explosion?"

"I almost wish it was only that."

Rathbone hesitated, reflectively stroking his beard.

"Something just as unexpected as an explosion. I'd better tell about it from the beginning.'

I half fell out of bed in my excitement.

"Two or three days after your disappearance on that crazy bear hunt, I was in my laboratory at the power plant. Suddenly I was shocked to see two men stagger in. They were both unnerved, one of them all burnt and cut about the lips and cheeks, and the other blue in the face and gasping. 'What in heaven's name!' I yelled. But they were so blamed excited all they could do was stammer like half-wits—something about the pit.

"Without waiting to know more, I grabbed my fur coat and rushed ahead of them into the storm. Somehow I got to the pit, and down to the elevator entrance, where I saw another worker, also blue in the face, and gasping so I was afraid he'd suffocate. However, I was in too much of a hurry to stop. The elevator stood open just before me, and I wanted to murder that slouch of an Allenham for not being at his post. But there being no time to waste, I ran the car myself. As I popped into it, I noticed a peculiar acrid odor, but was too excited to pay much attention. However, I ought to've taken warning. When I threw the door open at the three-hundred-yard level, I was hit by that same acrid odor in a burst that, I tell you, nearly knocked me off my feet—a penetrating, stifling gas, which tore at my throat and nostrils so that for a moment I couldn't get my breath.

"Luckily, I had the presence of mind to slam the elevator door and pull the lever. But even after stepping out on the upper platform, it was a long while before I stopped gasping. I was told that my face, as I panted and coughed, had a bluish tinge."

"Holy saints! What was it, Steve?"

Rathbone let a grim smile lighten his furrowed features.

"That was one of the few questions I could answer. You'd have recognized that gas from its symptoms, Rod. It was unmistakable—our old friend, sulphur dioxide."

Of course I was familiar with this gas, whose fumes, in small quantities, cause the unpleasant odor of burning sulphur matches, and whose noxious torrents sometimes issue from volcanoes. A deadly fear clutched at me.

"You haven't explained how the dioxide got into the pit."

"No, I haven't. I ought to mention, however, that it wasn't our only unwelcome visitor. There were minute quantities of steam, which quickly condensed or froze; also, the typical rotten-egg odor of hydrogen sulphide; and various chlorine compounds, some of them poisonous. Or, rather, I should say there still are such vapors."

"You still haven't said where all those nice visitors came from."

Rathbone's prominent yellow-white teeth, showing just a touch of gold to the left, bit somberly into his lower lip.

"That's what I asked myself, Rod. But we got the explanation soon enough. Several eyewitnesses testified that a discharge of tri-nitro-fluoric acid had just been made into the pit. Suddenly, near the tunnel floor, they saw a violent eruption, looking a little like steam from an exhaust valve. Probably there actually was some steam in the mixture. But the more dangerous gases were there too, and its wasn't a minute before the workers, choking and gasping, were making a panicky exit. It's a miracle they all got away, considering how that rat Allenham quit the elevator at the first alarm."

"Any of them badly hurt?"

Rathbone groaned.

"Eleven. As bad luck would have it, Norwood, McDougal, and Kenworthy all happened to be in the pit inspecting. They're all in bed now from the poisoning. Oh, don't look so disturbed, Rod," Rathbone reassured me, smiling wanly. "They'll all recover, though the ones nearest the outburst were pretty severely burned by the boiling-hot fumes. Dr. Straub, with Ada's help, was splendid at first aid."

"Well, after all, it's only half a disaster," I consoled him glumly. "But how will you expel the gases from the pit?"

"That's the question, Rod. First of all, it's necessary to understand their origin."

"And you don't understand?"

"I believe I do."

He paused, and my ghastliest fears were reinforced.

"Remember a discovery we made right after coming here? About the lava fields, and Kenworthy's conclusions that Devil's Peak is an extinct volcano? Well, the indications now are it's not extinct."

"Not extinct?"

"Oh, don't be alarmed," counseled Rathbone, though he didn't seem adept at taking his own advice. "There isn't much chance of an eruption. Still, the gases in the pit do show active volcanic forces at work."

"How do you know?"

"Well, you haven't forgotten the common theory of volcanic eruptions," Rathbone hastily went on. "It used to be held that the magma, or molten rock, composed largely of iron and silicates, underlies the crust everywhere at about forty miles. A more recent belief is that the earth is solid, with layers of rock above a hard, metallic center. But under any theory, the earth can't be absolutely all solid, since heated liquids and gases do well up toward the surface in volcanoes, geysers and hot springs. So it's believed there are fissures through

which this hot matter wells up. When it comes within
a few miles of the surface, the reduced pressure re-
leases the gases held in solution in the viscid matter
or magma. These gases make their way to the roof of
the fissure, and gather there in enormous quantities,
until the power of their compression makes them act
like an overheated boiler."

"In other words, they explode."

"Yes. They shatter the shell above them in a volcanic eruption."

"And you think, Steve, we're near one of these great
rents in the earth's crust?"

"I'd say there's a vast storehouse of molten rock not
many miles under us. I haven't the faintest doubt this
caused the former eruptions of Devil's Peak. This, also,
has given rise to gases that have seeped under the island
through tiny cracks and crevices."

"Your point, then, is that our excavation, by some
unlucky chance, ran into one of those cracks or crevices?"

"Yes, by some hellish stroke of luck. Besides, there
are other facts to back this view."

Rathbone had arisen, and stood looking down at me
severely, his hands clasped together behind him.

"Well, here's something I hadn't wanted to mention

before. You know that, judging from observations elsewhere, we had a right to expect that the temperature would rise one degree Fahrenheit for every fifty or sixty feet we dug down. Yet at the three-hundred-yard level, the temperature has averaged twenty-two degrees higher than at the surface—almost one degree for every forty feet! It was the same, if not worse, at the nine-hundred-yard level. The gain there was a fraction over sixty-eight degrees—a slightly higher rate than up above. Now what would you suppose that indicated, Rod?"

"Well," I reasoned, "I'd say there's something pretty hot underneath."

"Something exceptionally hot!" emphasized Rathbone. "In other words, a great fissure in the earth's crust, with the white-hot magma a comparatively short distance below."

"Better get down on your knees and give thanks," I advised, despite the sickly feeling within me. "Isn't that just what you wanted, Steve? Now you won't have to bore so far down to get heat enough to reclaim the island."

"Hope you're right," mumbled Rathbone, pursing up his lips doubtfully. "But why not be frank with ourselves? It could imply just what you say, Rod; or it could involve no end of troubles."

Rathbone gritted his teeth, clenched his fists, and stood staring at me and past me with the defiant look I had once seen in a captive tiger.

"We've got no choice but to keep on—keep on with all that's in us. We've got to fight to the last man and the last flicker of energy, and forget those devils' fires sizzling just under our feet. The first thing, therefore, will be to clear the pit of poison gas."

"Any way you know of doing that?" I shot out, my head aching. "From the way you talk, it would be death even to enter the tunnel."

The old Rathbone confidence had begun to reassert itself.

"So it would be—if you entered unprotected. However, I'm working on a scheme"—he paused, and smiled in the old reassuring way—"a scheme that may rid us of the gases. Maybe it'll be dangerous, but it'll be worth trying."

Bending down with a quick gesture, Rathbone took my hand and announced, "Now, Rod, I'd better get along!"

With a wave and a nod he was gone. But I was haunted by visions of flaming geysers, red volcanic cones, and fires that spattered crimson through the night.

XII

A few hours later, I was awakened out of a deep sleep. It seemed that something had seized me by the shoulders and was shaking me; my first impression was that an enemy had attacked. Then, as I stared about me in instinctive terror, the shaking momentarily ceased, but was renewed in a single sharp jolt, while the walls rattled and a glass of medicine fell with a crash from a chair at my side.

For minutes I lay shuddering. Had there been an explosion at the power plant? Or had the gases at the pit broken loose?

It was Rathbone who, an hour later, confirmed my worst suspicions.

"Well," he demanded, bursting into my room, "feel the earthquake?"

"Should say I did. First and worst I ever went through."

"Let's hope it'll be the first and the last, Rod. Luckily, it didn't do much damage. What bothers me is the cause."

"You mean—the volcanic furies under the island?"

He nodded glumly.

"But isn't it believed, Steve, that most earthquakes are not due to volcanoes, but to readjustments in the earth's crust?"

"True! Yet some earthquakes are of volcanic origin. Everything leads me to conclude this one belongs to that class. Some sort of disturbance is evidently going on right beneath our feet."

I groaned. "Nothing dangerous, I hope?"

"Not necessarily. The quake may have been the work of pent-up gases and fluids, which will remain pent-up. Just the same"—Rathbone paused, and waved one hand as if wishing to dismiss the subject—"there's no telling positively."

His shoulders hunched just a little, he hastened away, so preoccupied that he forgot to say "goodbye."

A few days later, a typed notice was posted in every house:

"EVERYBODY LOOK—IMPORTANT!

"I will expect all those not on the sick list to be in my office in the power plant this afternoon at two.

Stephen Rathbone."

Since all but three victims of the fumes were now well enough to attend, there were seventy persons at the meeting—so many that the collapsible partitions separating four rooms had to be removed and the whole opened into a fair-sized hall.

Rathbone waited for the last of us to arrive, then with a determined, almost martial stride, stepped to the front. Our eyes now had no target but that broad-shouldered, bull-faced man.

He lifted one short thick hand, with the index finger pointed upward; cleared his throat and began:

"Friends, probably you've guessed why I've called you here. There's no use beating around the bush; fact is that we're face to face with a crisis. It's a crisis that we'll have to fight all together; otherwise, we're licked from the start. So I'm going to ask for your undivided help. It has come to my ears that some of you have been grumbling. I don't want to be harsh; I know just what you've had to put up with. On the other hand, I will not and cannot stand for disaffection or treachery. I *will not* and cannot! Therefore, if anyone has any just complaint, let him stand up and mention it!"

Rathbone had gradually raised his voice almost to a shout. Now, when he lapsed into silence, the quiet seemed ominous.

Several feet were heard shuffling uneasily.

"As I've just said," he resumed, lowering his voice, "we're all in peril, and any act against our common aim is a crime against us all. I have no choice but to suppress such crime with all means at my disposal. Thus far, I'm happy to report, there has been only one occasion for punishment. One of you, who deserted his post at a critical moment, has been mildly chastised. I consulted Dr. Straub before prescribing the punishment, and he reported that the culprit would probably be benefited rather than harmed by ten days on half-rations."

A wave of laughter rippled around the room. I noticed how one man's face colored, and how his head bent low to avoid our amused, contemptuous glances.

"I don't regard the punishment as cruel," Rathbone continued. "Besides"—he raised one hand authoritatively, checking another burst of laughter—"this man is only practicing a skill that all of us may have to develop before the winter's over.

"This, however, isn't what I called you here to discuss. I have in mind something of immediate interest, which need concern only brave men. If any of you would rather not face hardship and danger, I'll give you time to leave this room at once."

Rathbone paused. But all sat statue-still.

"Then I take it," he proceeded slowly, "that no one here is afraid of hardship or danger. Splendid! You all know of the poison gases in the pit, and the halt in our work. This has lasted two weeks already; all that time, I've been busy with a plan for getting rid of the vapors. One or more of us must go down into the pit, equipped with small water tanks, a breathing outfit and a welding apparatus, and try to seal the fissure, which doesn't appear to be very large. A gas mask will protect the wearer from the poison fumes; a wire from above will carry a current to dissociate the water in the tank by a process of electrolysis, the hydrogen being liberated and the oxygen kept for breathing. The same wire, incidentally, will enable the man to signal in case of need. I've already completed several of the contrivances. Here! I'll show you!"

Stepping to one side, Rathbone unlocked a cabinet, and drew forth a contraption that looked like a diver's suit. He immediately slipped on a mask that made him resemble some grotesque beetle; mantled his limbs in a dark, canvas-like substance; and strapped upon his back a pail-sized metal tank penetrated by a tangle of wires and rubber tubes.

"I've adapted this from some old diving suits we had brought along, just in case of need," he explained, after stripping off the apparel. "The total weight is sixty-two pounds which is less than the wartime pack of many soldiers. As for the garments—they're composed of a specially prepared wool-asbestos composite, which is such a poor heat conductor that it will protect the wearer from the hot vapors at the pit bottom. Thus, as you'll see, I've taken every precaution. Nevertheless, it's only fair to warn you again that there are risks. So I'm not asking anyone to go unwillingly; I'm calling for volunteers. As Volunteer Number One, I name myself."

Again Rathbone paused, and again a hush fell upon the gathering. I could hear a heavy breathing behind me. McDougal, to my left, had turned pale. Ada, at the further end of the row, looked up at her brother with admiring wide eyes from which she hastily brushed a tear.

"I'm ready for other volunteers!" announced Rathbone.

"Count me Number Two!" boomed a voice to my

right.

A round of clapping burst out—cries of "Good for you, John!" and "Hurrah for Norwood!"

Norwood waited until the commotion had died down, and then, having risen to his feet, went on in his vibrant bass.

"I've got to enter a protest, Mr. Chairman, and I think everybody will bear me out. An expedition like ours can stand risking one or two of the rank and file. But if it lost its leader, it would be like a headless chicken. So I'm asking you to go back on your decision."

"Go back on my decision?" bellowed Rathbone.

"Yes, send all the rest of us privates into the pit, if you want. But stay out yourself. We need you here, and, by gum, we're going to keep you here! What do you say, boys?"

"Yes, yes, yes! . . . That's it! You're right, you're right! We want Mr. Rathbone here!" a dozen voices broke out.

"That's the way, boys! I knew how you'd feel!" Norwood thundered on. "It isn't as if the rest of us were trembling rabbits. Why, I can see that most of you are simply exploding to hand in your names!"

"You bet we are, John!" came the hearty voice of Andy McPherson from somewhere in the rear. "Call me Volunteer Number Three!"

"I'm fourth!" cried Jan Olafsen and I in one voice, as we leapt simultaneously to our feet.

"That's it; first-rate men, all of you!" approved Norwood. "Well, what do you say, Mr. Chairman?"

"I agree they're all first-rate men," concurred Rathbone. "I must say you've got an unholy nerve, John, but if I try to put myself in your place I can see some sense in what you say. I consent to removing my name to the list of alternates."

XIII

"No use jeopardizing any more of you than we have to," Rathbone decided at a meeting of the volunteers. "It looks to me as if one man, with luck, might be able to seal up the fissure, so I'm going to send you down singly."

"How about letting me first try?" I requested.

"How about me?" came three other voices.

"Fairest way will be to draw lots," proposed Rathbone, as he prepared four bits of paper, numbered from 1 to 4, each looking precisely like the others.

"Suppose you draw first, John."

Norwood snatched at one and growled an oath. "Hang it all, just my luck!"

Gloomily he displayed number 4.

"You next, Olafsen."

Olafsen plucked at the second straw, and surveyed

it with a pleased look. It was number 2.

"Now you, McPherson."

Something caught at my throat as McPherson reached for the straw. Suddenly by some eerie intuition, I knew that matters of life and death were at stake.

After several slow seconds, he exhibited his paper, scrawled with the figure 1.

Yet he did not seem jubilant, even when Rathbone congratulated him.

An hour or two later, an excited group gathered in the scourging cold near the pit. By this time McPherson had regained his good cheer; there was an expectant grin on his bearded face as he donned his suit for the fifth or sixth time, listened to Rathbone's instructions.

"Go down as far as you can by elevator, McPherson. At the eight-hundred-yard level, leave the car, and descend the last hundred yards by the rope ladders. But don't forget: before you step out on the ladder, press the little button at your side, to signal us all goes well. If you're in danger, press the button three times. No matter what happens, don't stay at the bottom more than fifteen minutes. When you start back, press the signal button once more."

It was a queer procession that accompanied McPherson to the pit; all of us wore gas masks. We could not go as far as the pit itself, but stood a little way off to wish our comrade luck as, weighed down with his heavy garments, his metal tank and welding apparatus, he began to unwind the wire from a great coil, beckoned to us for the last time, and disappeared.

For the first minute or two the wire unwound rapidly; McPherson was making a swift, safe descent. After several minutes, we saw that it was moving more slowly, but were reassured when a little electric bulb behind the pit gave a flash of light, informing us that McPherson was at the eight-hundred-yard level. The next instant, the wire jerked violently, but, after a moment, it became motionless again. This made us a little apprehensive; but we took it for granted that McPherson had reached the bottom, and was at work sealing up the fissure.

There was nothing to do now but wait. Speechless in the bleak night, we paced moodily back and forth across the snow and ice, sucking in labored, scanty breaths.

Sixteen minutes, seventeen minutes, eighteen minutes! Clear and solemn, each gong beat announced the passage of an era. Nineteen minutes, twenty, twenty-one! Had McPherson forgotten his wrist-watch? Had it been damaged, and stopped? Gloomily we stared at one another through our isolating masks. Meanwhile an aloof, silent figure, pacing near the base of the funnel, spoke more eloquently than he realized by the jerky twists and convolutions of his hands.

Twenty-two minutes, twenty-three, twenty-four! Each gong stroke hit us like a blow. Surely McPherson would not willingly remain below so long!

It was after the twenty-fifth stroke that Rathbone reached his decision. Striding away from the pit, he motioned us to follow; then, at a safe distance, he swept the mask from features which, in the dim electric glow, appeared bluish white and haggard.

"No use waiting any longer!" he snapped, his teeth chattering. "Something's happened to McPherson. Maybe his mask didn't fit right. He may be gasping for help. If we wait any longer, it may be too late. Some-one else will have to go down."

For a moment, we stared at the speaker in a petri-fied silence. Then Olafsen's voice rang out crisply.

"My turn, boys! Give me the things!"

"Me, too!" I chimed in. "Two is better than one!"

I was astonished at the savagery in Rathbone's man-ner. "You wait your turn, Rodney!"

But I watched with an obsessing anxiety as Olafsen

adjusted his asbestos clothing. Everything was done with the utmost speed; within five minutes Olafsen, in his diver-like costume, beckoned as McPherson had done, began to unwind a coil of wire, and disappeared into the shadows.

"If you need help," Rathbone instructed, "signal twice. If you find McPherson, signal four times."

But Olafsen signalled neither four times nor twice as the minutes went by. As before, the wire uncoiled rapidly; as before, an electric flash told that our comrade had reached the eight-hundred-yard level; as before, that flash was followed by a violent jerk upon the wire; and, as before, a silence settled down, while each gong beat struck us with new peals of alarm.

Five, six, seven, eight, ten, in a slow tantalizing succession; I seemed to be hearing the repeated strokes of doom. Even as the twelfth gong beat rang out, and the thirteenth, fourteenth and fifteenth, no welcome figure shot up from the pit entrance. Still we did not speak, for again we wore our gas masks as we clustered near the pit, stalking back and forth across the snow in a nervous, jerky way, starting at every shadow, and pausing to listen at each fresh sounding of the gong.

The twentieth gong signal, had just dinned when Rathbone again strode away from the pit, flung off his mask and summoned us to him.

"Same abominable thing all over again!" he grieved. "I can't understand it, simply can't. They've both reached the eight-hundred-yard level. Between there and the bottom something's happened. But what? God in heaven, what? Olafsen's mask was well adjusted—I examined it myself. If he's in trouble, why doesn't he signal?"

For one instant, by some trick of the pale yellowish light, Rathbone's face looked to me infinitely worn and old.

"Both of them must have been hit by something swift and sudden," he went on blankly. "But what? Can any of you, for God's sake, tell me what?"

A moment's silence followed. Then, with the feeling of one who drapes a shroud about his own shoulders, I tried to do my duty.

"Well, Steve, now it's my turn."

He flared up like a wind-whipped flame.

"It's your turn when I say so! Devil take you, d'ye think I want to risk any more lives? No, let's look over our plans, and see just what's slipped up."

"Think we've got all week ahead?" a booming voice broke out. And Norwood burst forward, waving his arms emphatically toward the pit. "Why, man, don't you realize, right at this minute two of the boys may be struggling for dear life in the pit. So let's not stand here arguing!"

"How do you expect one man to rush to the rescue?"

"Who said anything about one man? Lord, haven't we seen what happens when one goes alone? Two are more than twice as strong. Rod and I are next on the list, so why in blazes shouldn't we go together? Come on, Rod! Let's hop into our suits!"

"Not so quick there!" Rathbone protested. "We've lost two men with rope ladders. We're going to make some wire ladders before another man goes down into the that pit."

In two days, the new ladders were ready, and we set out.

XIV

It is no wonder that by the time we returned Norwood and I were regarded as dead men. We had been gone nearly three quarters of an hour; not a signal had come from us since we reached the bottom. During our absence, besides, an earthquake had occurred; the lighting apparatus had been disarranged above ground as well as beneath, and the frantic efforts to readjust it had resulted in a flickering, spasmodic illumination which had tormented us. Not until the moment of our reappearance had the equipment been put back in order. And the impossibility of entering the pit without light had delayed all attempts at rescue.

But now that a double miracle had taken place; now that we had returned alive after fulfilling our mission of sealing the fissure, sudden wild jubilation broke out. The men, too long restrained, shouted their joy to the frigid skies. For the first time in weeks, we saw smiling faces. All that remained to be done before operations were resumed was to remove the lingering gases from the pit by means of chemical solvents.

As a precaution, Dr. Straub ordered Norwood and me to rest for a day or two. The period, however, protracted itself into three or four days before we were pronounced ready for work again.

By this time our activities were going ahead once more. Reducing the work force at the power plant and foundry, Rathbone had assigned every available man to the pit; had begun to work the men in three shifts, never leaving the pit idle except on our one weekly holiday. Thanks to such adroit generalship, the bore deepened at astonishing speed: from nine hundred yards to twelve hundred and fourteen, until at length, amid general rejoicing, we celebrated our arrival at the one-mile mark.

Meanwhile the elevator shaft almost kept pace with the pit. Since we had no cable that would lift a car a mile, we built several elevators to occupy the shaft at different levels. These cars, turned out in the foundry, were taken in segments to the desired levels and there put together.

Unfortunately, however, not all went according to schedule. One thing continued to arouse our alarm. Rathbone expressed a general feeling one day just after we had reached the mile level.

"Know what the temperature readings are now, Rod?" he shot out at me, when I found him brooding over a chart in his office.

"No, all I know is that it's devilishly cold up above! A mild forty below, I'd say."

"Just about. Well, at the mile level it's ninety-four above. Ninety-four degrees Fahrenheit, Rod. That's pretty hot."

I made a rapid mental calculation.

"About a hundred and thirty-four degrees above surface temperature."

"Exactly! That's a trifle over one degree for every forty feet of descent. Well, you can figure for yourself, Rod. The temperature rise is twenty-five to fifty percent greater than expected."

He pushed the chart aside, snatched at a pack of documents, then went on, "Afraid we'll have to delay operations in the pit just a little. You know how bad the air's been getting, in spite of all our high-power fans and forced air circulation. Also, as I've pointed out, it's hotter than a man can properly work in, and getting worse. We'll have to go down as you know, till we reach boiling point; and if we don't want to be stewed alive, we'll have to keep the temperature in the pit far below that."

"Didn't you mention something about a system of pipes and electric pumps?"

"Yes, I've had it in mind to install a new system, driving the cold surface air into the depths at a rate regulated through a series of valves and automatic exhausts. Thus we'll have an air-conditioned, thermostatically regulated temperature no matter how far down we go. See, Rod, here are the plans."

By slow, too slow degrees, the year advanced, until once more the sun shone most of the day and night, the snow began to melt on the tundra, the gray fields of lichens and occasional green patches of grass appeared, and here and there some blue or golden wild flower flaunted defiance at the stern gods of the north.

You would have thought that we would have greeted the warmer season with songs and paeans. Yet it was as if the summer carried its own terrors; we knew how short it would be, and with what ferocious swiftness it would be followed by the time of gales, of sleet and snow. And now that we had lived through nearly a year on Icy Isle, there was something intolerable in the thought of another winter there.

Rathbone, as much as any of us, recognized just how we felt. And that was why he gave much thought and energy to a project which he had cherished ever since the loss of *The Comet:* the building of a short-wave radio transmitter. This involved extreme technical complexities, but fortunately McDougal and one or two of the other men were experienced at radio work. Not fully realizing the obstacles, I had at first expected an announcement from Rathbone before the winter's end, then by mid-spring, then in early summer. But June went by, and July, and part of August—and still the awaited tidings had not come. Ghastly premonitions began to haunt me: the grim phantom of approaching famine, and the specter of revolt. It was no longer easy to disregard the sullen faces, the looks of spite and hate, the whisperings and mutterings of secretive little knots of men.

On the eighth of August, Quin and I returned to

camp after a hunt on the island's further shore. As we came in sight of the settlement, the first thing we noticed was an unfamiliar structure, a sort of metal trellis carrying wires to a height of seventy or eighty feet above the powerhouse. A number of workmen, precariously perched on the steep powerhouse roof, were busily engaged in fastening down this metal structure.

When I reached the settlement, I was not surprised to see a typewritten notice on my door:
"MEETING TOMORROW MORNING AT NINE!
"At my office in the power plant. Everyone be present.
                                        Stephen Rathbone."

That night I did not sleep well. And next morning, when I arrived at Rathbone's office half an hour ahead of time, I had a heart-warming thrill. Facing me at the front of the room was a big, round, open-faced, wired steel contrivance. A microphone! A pledge of fresh contact with the world!

On a table beside the microphone, I saw another reassuring object: a short-wave radio receiver, the one that had come in *The Comet,* the only one not lost in that vessel's ill-fated last flight.

By the time we had all assembled, most of the men

were laughing, joking, and chaffing one another as they had not done for months. Ada, though thinner and more worn than a year ago, looked again her old exultant self; even Allenham, chatting at her side, appeared almost happy. But none of us quite realized the extent of Rathbone's accomplishment.

"Well, friends," he began with conversational simplicity, "I didn't want to call you here until I had something to show. You can hardly imagine the problems we've had to lick; if it wasn't for McDougal, I don't see how we could have won through. But I want you to see and hear for yourselves. Of course, you know we've been building a short-wave radio broadcaster. We've tried to make it as powerful as we could, and we're sure it will succeed, but we still haven't made any test. I want you all to share in that great moment."

Like an actor on a stage, Rathbone stalked back and forth.

"You realize, of course, that as far as our friends at home are concerned, we might as well have flown to Mars. They were never told where Icy Isle was; they've no way of knowing whether or not we reached it, or whether we're alive or dead. Therefore, until they have word of us, no help from them can be expected. My one regret is that it's already so late in the season. I feel certain, however, it's still not too late."

He turned to the microphone and made a few adjustments.

"Now don't be discouraged," he cautioned, "if we get no results at first. Under proper atmospheric conditions, our messages should carry three or four thousand miles; just the same, no one may be listening in on our wave length."

Seventy faces, tense and silent, stared eagerly at Rathbone.

"S. O. S.!" he called into the microphone. "The Rathbone Expedition. Sixty-eight men and three women marooned in the Arctic! Our dirigible has been destroyed. Our provisions are running low."

He turned several knobs, and a mumbling of static came to our ears.

"This is a powerful receiver," he explained, "but since it was just our luck to lose all the replacement tubes with *The Comet,* I've hesitated to use it when not strictly necessary."

The muttering of static continued.

"No one on our wave length!" he declared, after several minutes. "We'll try again."

And so, for the second time, he cried into the microphone, "S. O. S.! The Rathbone Expedition!" And, for the second time, we waited, greeted only by that idiot voice of static.

"S. O. S.! The Rathbone Expedition!" our leader repeated hoarsely. But still only that meaningless static! Someone coughed nervously. From the direction of "Sandy" Scruggs there came low, half-hysterical cackling laughter.

"S. O. S.! The Rathbone Expedition!" our chief exclaimed for the fourth time, the fifth, and the sixth. He was beginning to look grim; many faces were gray with disappointment.

Then all at once, above the static, some different sounds rose out of the receiver, wavered, and rose again.

In our excitement, we all sprang from our seats and started toward the instrument. But Rathbone, with an enraged gesture, motioned us back. Too late, we realized that our imbecilic noise had drowned out those precious radio sounds.

The next moment, the sounds were renewed, so low that Rathbone had to clap on headphones. A few long, breathless seconds followed. Then, in less time than it takes to jot down these words, the sounds had given place again to the low crackling of static. But Rathbone, snapping off the headphones, turned to us with eyes as wildly exultant as I have ever seen.

"The steamship *Columbia,* en route across the Pacific," he stammered, "has caught our message."

XV

Our rejoicing turned out to have been a bit premature. True, our plight and position had been made known to the world. But things worked more slowly than we had anticipated. Since we were not in immediate peril, plans for rescue moved with a deliberateness, a casualness that was maddening. The swift and only way obviously, was by air. But the swift and only way got snarled for precious weeks in red tape.

Since no private organization could provide the big long-range plans to help us, our appeal had been directed to Washington. But the civilian officials dropped the problem in the lap of the army, and the army played pushball with it for a few days, then passed it on to the navy, which passed it back to the army, which passed it to the air force. And all the while time was slipping by, and the brief bloom of summer was leaving Icy Isle.

Nevertheless, in anticipation of aid, Rathbone had commissioned a crew with a bulldozer to clear away a long patch on the most level part of the island as an airplane runway and landing strip. It took twenty men almost a month to complete this Herculean task. And no sooner had they finished the mile-and-a-half strip, which at this season we could keep mostly clear of ice, than galvanizing news reached us.

It was already the seventh of September, and I shivered in a heavy woolen sweater. I was just leaving the house for a hunt with Quin, when I was startled to hear a great shout from the gray world of drifting mist. The shout was repeated, accompanied by cheers, and a band of men broke into view from around a corner of the settlement, leaping and cavorting like Indians.

"What is it, boys? What is it?" I called.

As the men moved past, cheering and welling in an exultant serpentine, a figure detached itself from their ranks.

"Glory, haven't you heard, Rod?" demanded Norwood, rushing up to me and shaking both my hands. "The Secretary of Defense has given the order!"

"Order? What order?"

"For our rescue, of course! A B-36 leaves for Icy Isle on the tenth!"

"Thank God!" I muttered.

But somehow I was less enthusiastic than Norwood. "Only one plane, John, even a big one, won't solve our problem."

"Who said it would? But it's a peach of a beginning. It'll bring us several tons of concentrated food, also medical supplies. And those who don't want to stay will have their chance to leave."

"You're not one of those, John?"

His laughter smote me like a blow.

"Me? Count on me to hang on till the last seal leaves Icy Isle!"

"Me too, John, till the bananas ripen around Frost Lake."

"Good for you!" Norwood approved, again grasping my hand. And then, with a grimmer look, "However, you know blazing well not all the boys feel like we do. Can't say I really blame them, either. I can't help admitting there are moments when I too feel like flying away—going off somewhere where arc lights are glaring and music plays. It's just a phase, of course, and I get over it."

"Will Steve let anyone go back who wants to?"

Norwood nodded. "He knows it's no use holding any man against his will."

"How many do you think will leave?" I gasped, with an alarming vision of Icy Isle depopulated.

"Well, Steve was afraid the men might leave whole-sale," Norwood went on thoughtfully. "But I've gone among them, subtly planting the idea that only a yellow cur would desert at this stage. Of course, some will leave, no matter what you say. But I don't imagine there will be more than twelve or fifteen. Steve won't mind that many; it will lighten the food drain. Operations have reached the stage where we can get along with a few less."

Norwood's estimates turned out to be remarkably accurate. Later that day Rathbone called us all together, and stated that anyone who wished to return on the B-36 might hand in his name. And no more than fourteen stood up to proclaim that they had had enough of Icy Isle.

The last to announce himself had been wincing and fidgeting opposite me. Alan Allenham's face had appeared by turns flushed and pallid, and his fingers had clenched and unclenched as if seizing and releasing some invisible object. Finally he struggled to his feet.

With all eyes upon him, he falteringly began.

"I—I—all things considered, I haven't been any too well here. Besides, I—naturally, I don't want to go if I'm needed, but I don't see that I'm really much use to you."

He coughed; hesitated.

"I don't know, of course, exactly how she feels, but I'm hoping—well, I'm hoping the lady at my side will share my decision—"

On September ninth I visited Rathbone's office with the news that Quin and I, using one of the Eskimo canoes or "kayaks," had speared several large fishes— a welcome addition to our larder. Rathbone received the tidings with a smile, then pointed to some typed pages on his desk, and requested, "Do me a favor, Rod. Put up one of these sheets in each of the houses."

"Right away," I agreed, reaching for the papers and a box of thumbtacks, while my eyes ran along the announcement:

"NOTICE: Owing to mechanical difficulties, the flight of the B-36, according to a radiogram just received, has been postponed from the 10th to the 12th.

Stephen Rathbone."

"That's too bad!" I remarked, as I started from the room. "It's already so late in the season."

"Don't I know it?" grumbled Rathbone, with a helpless shrug. "But what can I do? If the machine isn't in condition, why in Pete's name don't they send another?"

In a dismal mood, I left for the houses, and in each I tacked a notice above the sitting room door. I had just entered the eleventh when suddenly I forgot my reason for coming.

Even as I stepped in; even as the outer door shut behind me, strange sounds reached me from beyond a closed partition. There was a gasp, then a clatter as of some small glass thing shattering, then a louder clatter, then another gasp, a half-choked scream, a noise as of scuffling and struggling.

While my papers fluttered to the floor, I banged the door open and burst into the room.

Instantly, it seemed, I was grappling with a tall, lanky man, whose cork-brown hair and beard were disheveled, whose long weaving fingers began to close about my throat. Beside us, gasping for breath, her hair also disheveled, her clothing rumpled, a ragged rip in her plaid woollen blouse, and red contusions about her throat, a woman reeled and tottered.

It may have been her screams that brought help as my antagonist and I rolled over and over on the floor, while his hands clawed closer, closer about my throat. Meanwhile, I had the sensation of choking, as in my climb from the vapor-filled pit. It was as if snake-bands were winding about my throat, squeezing, squeezing, squeezing. . . .

Then all at once the snake-bands uncoiled. I drew in a great painful breath; and struggling back to my feet out of the ruins of an overturned bureau and chairs, I saw three crimson-faced men holding down my opponent, whom I recognized as "Sandy" Scruggs. At the side, one hand clutching at her breast, Ada stood, blue eyes wide with horror.

Scruggs, cursing and muttering, meanwhile was gripped to the cot by three glowering adversaries.

"Better call Mr. Rathbone," one of them suggested.

In a surprisingly short time, a panting and fiery-faced Steve burst into the room.

At a glance, he took in the situation. "Lord! What's the meaning of this?" he demanded. And he peered at his sister with tenderness and concern. "Not hurt, Ada?"

"No, I'm all right," she answered with an effort.

Meanwhile Rathbone had faced the author of the trouble.

"Scruggs," he said severely, "in other places and circumstances, this would be a hanging offense. I could hardly blame the boys if they strung you up. On the other hand, I think your trouble is pathological. You're a sick man, so I'm not going to punish you as most folks would say you deserve, but I'm going to see that you don't attack anyone else. Until the B-36 arrives, I'll keep you under guard in your room. When it comes, you can pick up your things and step aboard."

The pinioned man uttered a fearful curse.

But Rathbone, ignoring his mumblings, ordered a guard posted in front of his door; then started away, arm in arm with Ada. "Better step in to Dr. Straub's, Sis," I heard him saying, "just to make sure those wounds on your throat won't give you any trouble." And then to me, as he saw how blue with bruises I also was, "Come along, Rod. Looks like you can stand some treatment yourself."

XVI

By a special order of our leader, September twelfth was a holiday in camp. The pit and the power plant lay idle; the foundry and the coal mine were deserted. Most of us joining in a ceremony of rejoicing, skipped about the gray mossy tundra like ten-year-olds, played gypsy-like games, or improvised dances to the tunes of a flute which one of the men had unearthed. It seemed to me that I was alone in feeling a heaviness at the pit of the stomach.

One of our popular recreations, on this gala day, was to listen to reports of the airplane's progress. It was to leave early that morning from a Pacific Coast airport, and would reach Icy Isle at about four in the afternoon, so as to permit it time to land before sunset. Its non-stop flight was followed constantly at the radio by Rathbone and others, who received reports at fifteen-minute intervals. "Now it's over Seattle!" they would announce. . . . "Now above Vancouver Island. . . . Now in sight of Queen Charlotte Island. . . . Now over the Gulf of Alaska, approaching Seward. . . . Now almost at Nome. . . . Now beyond Nome, beginning to cross the Arctic. . . ."

As the final hours of our long wait dragged out, I tried to forget my growing uneasiness, my dread, by mingling with the crowd about the radio in Rathbone's office. Twelve or fifteen of us, including Norwood and Kenworthy, were sitting or standing there. A microphone was at one side; McDougal, seated before the radio, was listening through headphones, as was Rathbone, at his left.

For nearly fifteen minutes I stood waiting in silence.

"About time for another message, isn't it? I asked, edging up to Norwood.

"Just about," he admitted, biting into his lower lip. "Last we heard, they were running into stiff head winds."

Rathbone, at this point, relieved himself of the headphones.

"We've just heard again," he reported. "They're about seven hundred and forty miles south southeast. They think they can beat the gale by rising to thirty thousand feet."

At the next announcement, fifteen minutes later, the B-36 had altered her course slightly to avoid a rain-squall. She was now flying above the clouds.

Another tense hour followed; then the vessel reported herself within four hundred and fifty miles. And as the news traveled about the island, we could hear shouts of rejoicing.

Stepping out for a breath of air, I was a little disturbed to see one of the sea fogs, so common in this region, rolling in across the ice floes. This would spoil our view of the approaching airplane; nevertheless, in this age of radar, it would not greatly matter.

But when I returned to Rathbone's office half an hour later, I detected a change of mood. The watching crowd, grown to twenty, was even tenser than before; but their eyes did not gleam any more; most of them stared in bleak silence at the solemn two with the headphones.

"What's happened?" I asked Norwood.

He seemed not to hear me.

Five minutes went by. Then Rathbone, his face almost white, again slipped off the headphones.

"Things look a bit better now," he stated, in a manner of crisp reassurance. "They're working at that balky engine—think they'll have her back in no time."

A sudden giddiness made me clutch at a chair for support. I had visions of a lonely plane, far out over the ice-littered Arctic, as it staggered on against head winds with a crippled engine.

"If it weren't too far," Rathbone stated, in a tone meant to be calm, "they'd turn back to Nome. But being nearer to Icy Isle, they've got to keep on."

No one attempted to reply. Another quarter of an hour, and another, dragged on. The radio messages, still coming at regular intervals, told us that the ship was continuing northward at reduced speed; the damaged engine remained cold, but the crew was still working hard to restore it to action. By five thirty at the latest, they would be over Icy Isle.

This would be nearer to sunset than we had wished. But the all-important fact was that the rescuers were approaching.

And so, in successive reports, the news came that they were only two hundred miles away, only a hundred and fifty, only a hundred, only fifty! Now all of us, with a few exceptions, thronged toward the landing strip.

But I, strapped down as by a spell, lingered among the four or five watchers about the radio. Still another fifteen minutes went by; Rathbone and McDougal remained glued to the headphones. What was it that they had heard?

"Not a thing!" Rathbone answered our unspoken questions without removing the headphones. "Not a thing! I just can't understand it!"

Clustered about the radio with strained faces, we remembered those dreadful hours last year when we awaited *The Comet's* final return.

Five minutes more went wearily by. Ten minutes. Fifteen. . . .

"No, not a word," Rathbone repeated. "I can't understand it at all. They should have been here long ago."

Then suddenly he popped forward in his seat. His eyes seemed to bulge out of his face. His lips drew wide. In a dead, lifeless manner, he uttered three syllables. "S. O. S."

Even before the shock of that announcement had sunk in, a great shouting and clamoring sprang up from outside. And as we dashed out, still another noise came to our ears: a fierce whirring and buzzing, as of some gigantic insect in trouble.

Surely the demons of the fog had set their stage with masterful design. For a gust from the sea swept a huge swath of mist away from Devil's Peak. And in that swiftly cleared patch of air, in the gathering twilight, we saw a monstrous flying thing looping and lunging as if doing a death's dance. It shot upward; seemed within inches of scraping the peak; shot frenziedly down again, and violently up. Then with the roar of its motors still in our ears, it was lost behind another fog veil.

A few seconds later, the fog parted again and we had a glimpse of the black-winged shape spiraling as if out of control above the sea ice beyond the island shore. Then the fog closed again. The droning grew remote, and died out. And the crowd of us, in the cold fog as the twilight deepened, stood there and shivered, shivered and waited, and had no word aside from our low cries of dismay as we listened to the crunching of the ice blocks and the senseless beating of the waves against the shore, and knew how lost souls feel when abandoned by man and God.

XVII

After the loss of the B-36, Rathbone exchanged messages with Washington. He urged the immediate dispatch of rescue planes to save any possible survivors of the plane; and he appealed for fresh aid for ourselves, pleading that our position during the winter would be desperate unless we had help. I could understand the reluctance of the officials to risk further planes and lives; and I could see that, from their point of view as they sat in comfortable chairs in pleasant sunlighted offices, it was reasonable to hold back the decision for another day. But to us the delay was a thing of terror.

Next day, however, Rathbone brought us a heartening announcement. He was jubilant as he informed us. "The Air Force has commissioned a fleet of six planes to look for the lost vessel and send us aid. They leave tomorrow."

"You mean they'll bring us provisions?"

"Not only that, but they'll evacuate those who want to leave."

"But, Lord, we haven't landing facilities for six planes."

"Don't I know that? They'll have to come in one at a time, discharge their baggage, and set off again in a jiffy."

And so once more there was rejoicing in camp, though mingled with a hard undercurrent of skepticism. "Well, maybe those planes are coming, but we'll believe it when they land," Kenworthy expressed the general incredulity.

This feeling found support in the turn of the weather. Following the fog, a frigid blast blew down from the Pole; clouds swept across the sky; and a scanty dry snow began to fall. In such weather, obviously, it would be impossible to search for the lost plane; and in view of the iced condition of our runway it would be dangerous for any plane to land. And so Rathbone reluctantly radioed that, for the present, the planes should be kept in their hangers.

For five days the storm continued; and not until the twentieth of September, when a blue sky shone above a white earth, did Washington finally give the

order for the flight. On the morning of that day, Rathbone posted an announcement that the planes were
on the way; but most of the men, chilled by disappointment, merely shook their shoulders with a "so what?"
attitude.

Nevertheless, the planes did wing their way across
thirty-five hundred miles of sky. They did arrive not
far from Icy Isle, though we knew of their coming only
by radio; they did search the sea ice for the vanished
men; and they did send in the report we had dreaded
and expected: not a trace of the missing ones! Having
covered hundreds of square miles, they had to abandon
their efforts because of the fog that still blanketed
the area.

A little later, we again heard the welcome drone of
motors in a tremendous buzzing chorus while our
visitors circled above the island. As the news spread,
we all rushed outdoors—all except Rathbone and Mc-
Dougal, who remained faithfully at the radio. But the
ironies of Icy Isle were never-ending. We could hear
but could not see the rescuers!

The landing field, otherwise indistinguishable from
the surrounding country in its icy whiteness, had been
marked off by red flags and flares, which, we had hoped,
would help pilot the planes to a safe descent. Their com-

mander, however, thought otherwise. "You haven't the instruments to guide us," he radioed. "We would have to rely upon radar, which would show us the ground, but not the landing strip. Besides, it would be unsafe to linger. The ice is gathering dangerously on our wings. Instead of landing, we will drop the provisions."

Thus we learned that we would be icebound for another season.

In any case, provisions, life-saving provisions, would be showered down. On Rathbone's order, we all fled indoors, lest someone receive a packing crate on the head; then, while the planes droned above, portentously loud and near but still unseen, the rain of food-stuffs began.

A minute later, I heard the thud of something big and heavy on the ground just outside; and scornful of the risk, dashed out to investigate. Several men joined me from the house next door, and stood with me before the crate, which had split open, its dozens of small cans scattered in the snow. But their groans of disgust could be heard even above the rumbling of the planes. The crate was filled with tinned dog food!

However, being responsible for a team of Eskimo huskies, I was not unhappy about this gift.

A few minutes later, as the roar of motors began to

recede, the whole community rushed out to inspect the loot. Several men, seeing a large carton being washed about just offshore, waded into the icy waters, and cursed as they drew out a case of ruined cigarettes. Others rescued bags of coffee, of doubtful value after its submersion. Still farther out one or two cases sank before we could get to them. But the remainder of the provisions was eventually reclaimed. Dried beans and flour; canned beans with pork; canned soup, canned and dried milk, rice, chocolate, ham and bacon—these constituted the bulk of our additions. The total, we estimated, amounted to more than twelve tons.

"With luck, and by eating as sparingly as monks," Rathbone announced, after taking stock of our provisions, "maybe we can pull through till spring." But he spoke without his customary conviction; his eyes gleamed with the wistfulness of one who juggles a hope.

XVIII

One morning in November, I was awakened by cries of excitement. Men were scurrying in all directions; searching eyes were anxiously peering into the houses and out into the darkness of the snow fields. "Bellows! O'Malley! Scruggs!" eager shouts rang forth.

While I was wondering what this meant, a fur-clad form burst in breathlessly at my door.

"Mister Rodney! The dogs! They gone!" broke out my Eskimo partner Quin. "Bad man, he take them! They run away while we sleep! He take sledge, too!"

"God Almighty! What bad man took them?"

"Not all the dogs!" shouted back Quin, holding up one hand, and two fingers of the other. "One half! The other team still here! Three bad men, they go with dogs. They rob storeroom, and they go!"

"The dirty thieves!" I muttered, still but half able to

believe Quin's story. "Where'd they go?"

Quin threw up his hands helplessly.

Before I had had the chance to cross-examine Quin, another form came lunging out of the gloom. Even by the pale electric light, I could see how like a ghost's Rathbone's face had become, how his mittened fists fluttered, how his teeth bit into his bearded lip.

"Rod!" he launched out, in a quick staccato. "A dastardly thing's happened. That coward Scruggs has run away! So have Bellows and O'Malley! The loons want to make it back to civilization. But they'll only find icy graves unless we stop them. So hurry, you and Quin! Hitch up the other team! They can't be far yet—their tracks are easy to follow!"

"We'll make a speed record!" I agreed as I started for my things.

With a hasty gesture, Rathbone motioned me back.

"Norwood, Kenworthy and Knowlson will accompany you with rifles," he added. "Best not take any chances with men in their state of mind. If you don't overhaul them in half a day, let them go and head straight back to camp. Can't throw good men away for gangsters!"

We knew that the fugitives could not move rapidly, for Bellows was the only one of the three who had ever had anything to do with dog teams. We knew also that it was imperative to bring them back, not only for their own sakes and because we needed the stolen dog team, but because of the moral effect their escape would have in camp. If these three succeeded in getting away, there would be nothing to discourage further insubordination.

With stern, set faces, we trudged silently beside the sleigh or behind it; while the dogs, in the prime of condition, kept us straining and panting to equal their five miles an hour. Surely Scruggs could not match our speed! Yet he must have reckoned with the certainty of pursuit, and have put as many miles as possible between us.

Therefore we turned to one another, amazed and incredulous, when after less than an hour, we heard familiar sounds from beyond a ridge of ice. Was that the barking of dogs? Or only an illusion of the weird, frozen solitude? But no! the sound was repeated, again and again, full-throated, sharp, unmistakable, while our own dogs burst into an answering pandemonium.

What could it mean? Certainly the runaways had not paused to make camp so near the settlement!

Already we had almost overtaken them; only a few hundred yards separated us from the ridge. We covered

the first part of the distance rapidly, Quin and I urging
on the dogs, our three escorts striding before us, heads
bent low, rifles in hand, for the barking of our own
dogs had advertised our coming, and we expected that
the runaways would either take flight or make violent
resistance. And so, as we drew near, we moved more
cautiously.

Approaching the ridge, Norwood motioned Quin and
me to remain behind with the dogs. Side by side with
Kenworthy and Knowlson, he crouched low on the ice,
creeping forward inch by inch, his rifle pointed, his
eyes searching every crevice of the uneven sea crust.
By the clear moonlight, the three men resembled
stalking beasts of prey. We could see how wary their
manner of hugging the sheltering ice-banks, how catlike and measured each slow lift and fall of a leg or
arm. At last, after long minutes, they mounted the
ridge, which was neither very steep nor high; and with
rifles poised, peeped across.

Quin and I, a hundred yards behind, shuddered for
their sakes, fearing a fusillade. But not in a thousand
tries could we have guessed the sequel. Norwood, instead of keeping to his concealment, shot up to his full
height and burst into laughter—bawling, gusty laughter,
in which Knowlson and Kenworthy joined.

Quin and I took this as our signal to follow them up the slope. And the view from the top sent us both into spasms.

Huddled together at the foot of the incline, the three fugitives stood with a woebegone look. Beside them was the sledge, wrong side up, with hundreds of pounds of canned pemmican, dried meat, furs, sleeping bags and miscellaneous provisions scattered in the snow. The dogs' traces were snarled and knotted; the seven animals made little more than one tangled furry heap.

Sullenly the runaways stared up at us.

"Well, well, boys, need some help?" Norwood bellowed, as he came down the slope. "Nice little smash-up you've got there! One of the neatest I've seen, and I've run into some dandies!"

The fugitives still glared.

"Yes, siree, I marvel how you've done it!" Norwood went on, in thundering glee. "Don't see how you could get things worse messed up if you'd tried."

While Norwood bent double again with laughter, Kenworthy pointed to Scruggs with a shocked cry. "Say, man, what's happened to your hand?"

All at once we noticed the red patch showing through the furred mitten of Scruggs' left hand.

Scruggs grunted and swore. "The filthy hounds! One

of the bitches nearly ate my hand off!"

The rest of us examined the wound—a long red superficial slash. "Advise you to get back to camp pronto," counseled Kenworthy, "and let Dr. Straub give first aid."

"Sure, guess that's the only stinking thing we can do," conceded Bellows.

An hour later, we had collected the remnants of the provisions, and were all on our way back to the settlement.

Even during this bitter period, work in the pit was proceeding. Less than three months after the disaster of the B-36, the shaft had almost reached the two-mile level, and the temperature, as registered by a thermometer buried in the rock, had risen to 212 degrees. We had gained the long-sought mark, the boiling point of water!

I remember the triumphant glow on Rathbone's worn face when he told me of this accomplishment; the momentary brilliance in his sunken eyes.

"Rod, we've almost won out!" he exulted, as he went down with me to display his accomplishment. "After next summer, when we've installed boilers in the pit and heated the waters of Frost Lake, we'll actu-

.

ally have reclaimed Icy Isle!"

I said nothing, for we were in the elevator, descending at a speed that discouraged conversation.

"Even if it's been a hard pull, Rod," Rathbone went on, when we got out on the platform below, "Just think! In a few years, green tassels of wheat and corn will be waving where all you can see today are ice-covered tundra! Thriving communities will begin to dot this island and the entire Arctic! For centuries to come, the world's surplus population will migrate to the Polar regions, and its surplus food be produced there! And the improvement will start within a year! We ourselves will bring it about, Rod! We'll be the pioneers!"

"You mean, Steve, *you* will be the pioneer—the chief one! You will go down in history as one of the great discoverers! Now that you've reached the end of your excavating—"

A thoughtful expression crossed Rathbone's face.

"I didn't say we'd reached the end," he answered, after brief hesitation, while the two of us stood looking down into the electrically lighted vastness of the pit's lower half-mile. "If necessary, we might do without any more excavating, since water at the pit bottom would reach the boiling point in time. On the other hand, if we dug down another four or five hundred feet, so as to bring the temperature ten or twelve degrees above boiling, the water would be heated much more rapidly. Come to think of it, Rod, wouldn't it be just plain silly to miss that opportunity? We have time in plenty before the ice melts next summer. And we have more than enough tri-nitro-fluoric acid."

I do not know why, but I felt a chill at these words. "Listen, Steve," I protested, "hadn't you better leave well enough alone? Why take unnecessary chances? Slower progress, and safer—"

"Safer?" he threw back at me, in a blast of scornful laughter. "Good Lord, Rod, you're getting to be a dyed-in-the-wool standpatter! Why, on that principle, would we ever have come here in the first place"

I knew that any explanation I made would sound silly. Yet, unaccountably, my uneasiness remained.

It would not be long before I felt a graver worry.

Several days later, when Quin and I returned from a seven hours' hunting expedition, we were aware of something wrong in camp. As we mounted a ridge of ice for our first view of the settlement, we saw that the pit funnel was dark and the usual lights connecting it with the powerhouse were out. Between the powerhouse and the settlement, on the other hand, the regular lights were burning, and, on the road between, one or two persons were moving in a great hurry.

"More trouble! Bad trouble!" proclaimed Quin in his usual laconic style. "Come! We go see!"

Not doubting that he spoke truly, I pushed on at his side. Upon reaching the powerhouse, I noticed a crowd hovering about Rathbone's office. The first to meet me was Ada, her face more pale and drawn than I had ever seen it before, her eyes red.

"Oh, Rodney, I'm glad you've come!" she welcomed me in the hall outside the office. "Steve's going to need every man!"

"In heaven's name, what's happened, Ada?"

Before she could answer, Rathbone came shouldering through the doorway, drawn by the sound of my voice. I had never known him to look more tense, not even on that terrible day when Olafsen and McPherson disappeared in the pit. Some sharp instrument seemed to have cut the lines that ran from the corners of both eyes down across his cheeks.

"Ah, Rod, just the man we've been waiting for!" he bawled his greeting. And then, with apparent irrelevance, "Any luck in the hunt?"

"Only one small rabbit."

"Well, a whale or two would come in handier," he

mumbled. "However, every morsel counts."

For a moment it seemed to me that his mighty strength was cracking. He threw out both hands and seized mine fervently.

"Tell me, Rod," he demanded, "tell me you're loyal, no matter what happens! Tell me you're loyal to the last ditch!"

"You know that, Steve. Could you ever doubt it?"

"I don't doubt it. Just the same, others that I didn't doubt have deserted like rats. There are just thirty-six of us left."

"What in creation are you talking about?"

"Come into my office, and I'll tell you."

Pushing our way inside, I saw Norwood seated at Rathbone's desk, telephone in hand.

"No! No! No!" he was barking. "You fellows have the wrong idea. If you don't forget all this baloney and come to terms before the chief gets real mad—"

Rathbone slumped down into a chair beside Norwood, while the latter roared to the end of his speech. The men were still crowding the room, and the atmosphere was hot and heavy.

"I've been giving them what for," Norwood informed us, as he turned from the receiver with a grin. "Only way to deal with such bandits. You know what's happened, Rod?"

"Sounds like some of the boys have revolted."

"Some of them?" sighed Rathbone. "Not just some of them! Half of them!"

I felt as if a hammer had pounded me on the head. "Oh, but that's impossible!"

He pursed up his lips wryly, and a hollow groan came forth. "It's always been my motto, Rod, nothing is impossible."

"But who's behind it all? Surely not Scruggs—you've got him under room arrest."

Rathbone turned upon me fiercely.

"I *had* him under room arrest, you mean! The vile blackguard escaped!"

"Bellows and O'Malley also escaped," added Norwood.

Out of sheer nervousness, Rathbone had arisen. One hand pounded the desk till the pine boards rattled.

"We're not quite sure of the details. Looks like they were in with the guards. We tried to pick jailors we could be sure of; but things are so abnormal now, every man nursing some morbid crazy grudge!"

"So the guards conspired to let the prisoners loose?"

"They let them loose, all right—don't know whether they conspired!"

"But how can three men cause so much trouble, even if they did get out?"

"Three men, you say?" Rathbone snorted, still hammering at the desk. "Wish it was only three! Remember how I commissioned ten of us to go hunting? I had a feeling against putting guns into so many hands, but what could I do? Starving to death wouldn't have been any remedy. Well, those outlaws, Scruggs, O'Malley and Bellows, no sooner broke loose than they fell in with four hunters just coming back from Devil's Peak. They got those fiends to join them, along with three more hunters, which, with the three armed guards, gave them thirteen men and a lot of rifles."

"But how did he persuade so many?"

"Persuade them? Why, a deaf mute could have done that. You know how the boys have been grumbling. They're so fed up with Icy Isle they're ready to follow a blind beggar."

"Where are they now?" I questioned, really alarmed.

"Wait, I'm coming to that. Before they got to their stronghold, they ran into ten more of the boys, or looked them up, I don't know which, and enlisted them. That made twenty-three, and as bad luck would have it, I was down in the pit bottom and hadn't any idea what was going on. By the time I got out, it was too late."

"What do you mean, too late?"

Rathbone stared at me dismally.

"Guess you understand English. Curse them all! They showed expert generalship. What happens to you in a war, Rod, if the enemy, in a surprise raid, captures your only source of supplies?"

"Why, you—you—I guess you give up," I answered stumblingly. "My God, Steve, they haven't — they haven't—"

"What makes you think they haven't? The whole bunch of them, the dirty thieves and cutthroats! made straight for two of the buildings. Numbers sixteen and seventeen!"

Once more I felt as if someone had slugged me on the head. Numbers sixteen and seventeen contained the storerooms and the communal kitchen and dining room.

"They've barricaded themselves in," Rathbone droned on drearily, "and nobody can get near unless he joins them. Well, I guess the stomach speaks loudest; that's why another dozen men have gone over, which leaves us only thirty-six, including Ada and me and the four Eskimos."

"What about Allenham?"

Rathbone glowered, and motioned me to silence. Glancing to one side, I saw Ada approaching from the corridor—and I thought I knew one reason her eyes were red.

"It's just the call of bread and meat," Rathbone continued sadly, lowering his voice. "Unless we do something, and mighty fast, I don't see how we can hold many of the remaining thirty-six."

XIX

Tired to the point of exhaustion, I was sleeping soundly. It seemed that my head had hardly touched the pillow when, in the midst of a dreamless slumber, I awakened abruptly, aware that the room was in violent motion. As if some tremendous invisible power had clutched the house, all things rocked, rocked, rocked dizzily, crazily, spasmodically in a series of sharp, irregular jerks. All the while, a terrific roaring was in my ears, the tumult of objects falling, the crashing and shattering of windows, shouts and shrieks, the barking of frightened dogs. As I lay huddled in the dark with a fast-pounding heart, the disturbance seemed never-ending.

Yet upon being jerked out of sleep, I had noticed that the radium-dial clock registered 6.01. And when the tremors ended, the time was only 6.02.

Even as I leapt out of bed, the shocks were renewed. Then came the most frightening crash of all, accompanied by the noise of a great tearing and rending. With bewildered eyes, I caught glimpses of the stars! And while an icy wind shot in, I saw how two of the walls had separated, leaving a gaping opening.

Terrorized, I reached for the electric push button. But it did not respond. And as I fumbled in the chilly gloom for my fur garments, the earth gave a last convulsive jerk and, to my enormous relief, became motionless.

Then, for the first time, I listened to the shouts that filled the air. "Hey, you, there! . . . Knowlson! . . . Rathbone! . . . Norwood! . . . My God! get me a light! . . . Anybody hurt over there? . . . Blast it, this wall's down!" In a confused chorus, yells of pain and terror burst over me. Almost at the same time, through the aperture in my wall, I saw oil lamps flaring, illuminating dark figures that shot past.

Fully dressed at last, I staggered into the open.

Except for one or two flickering lamps and the light of the half-moon, the settlement was almost in total darkness. The dim walls, beneath shadowy bluffs, looked out of position, twisted freakishly, or slanting like towers of Pisa. But what most astonished me was a red glow from the direction of the pit and the power plant.

In that first bewildering moment, I did not ask myself what this glow might mean. Now that my own immediate peril was past, a stabbing fear shot over me. What of my comrades?

"Ada! Ada!" I shouted, with acute alarm. But no one heeded, no one noticed how I stumbled across the frozen ground to her door.

As I drew near, the door burst open, and I saw her gliding toward me, candle in hand. Her clothes were thrown about her haphazardly.

"Rodney! Oh, I'm so relieved!" she cried, flinging out both arms to me. "Are you hurt?"

"No, I'm all right. How about you?"

"I—I guess I'm all right, too."

She was interrupted by a fresh shuddering of the ground.

"Seen Steve?" she asked with unconcealed anxiety, after the quake had ceased. But I barely had time to nod in the negative before the earth gave another sharp jerk.

For a tormented moment, we stood staring at one another hopelessly. The interval was made vivid by the shouting of men and the howling of dogs.

Then, in the dimness, she pointed along the row of

houses to the last one, the storehouse. Its roof had opened wide; its walls were twisted as if by an air bomb. Not until later, however, did I notice the ragged crack in the ground directly under the building.

In less than another minute—possibly in less than half that time—small knots of men had begun to gather in front of the houses, some of them swinging oil lamps, others picking their way with flashlights.

"Where's Bill? . . . Where's Ed?" I heard them crying. "Anybody hurt over your way? . . . My shoulder's bruised! . . . Lord, everything here's washed up. . . . This darkness is the devil! Can't anybody get the lights back again? . . . Oh, Lord, I got it right in the jaw!"

Amid the confusion, it was impossible to tell how many of us were there. But I thought I saw one or two of the rebels, including Bellows and Allenham.

"Rathbone! Where's Rathbone?" some of the men began to shout, in answer to Ada's repeated, "Where's my brother? Anybody seen my brother?" And sudden realization stunned us. Rathbone was nowhere in sight!

"Come; let's try all the houses," I suggested. And with Ada at my side and half a dozen of the men trailing after, we hastened from dwelling to dwelling.

In every building, some of the seams in the walls had come apart; in every building, the furniture lay heaped in confused masses. But still our leader was not to be seen.

"Rathbone! . . . Mr. Rathbone! . . . Where are you?" we shouted.

There was no answer. I began to shiver, not wholly with cold. Ada was shaking as if from the ague.

Finally, after we had visited the tenth house, a yell went up, and we saw two familiar figures swinging toward us around a bend in the headland to the east, Norwood dangling an oil lamp, his companion striding beside him across the hard snow.

"Calling me?" Rathbone demanded, in a quick, jerky manner, scarcely seeming to hear our exclamations of relief. "What is it? Anyone hurt? Ada, you all right? And you, Rod?"

Somehow we mumbled our replies.

"Sorry you couldn't find us," he rattled out. "John and I were up long before six—just in case. Been investigating that red light over in the east."

These words gave us no intimation of what was to follow. I had never heard a more sudden change in any man's tones, or seen a face more convulsed than Rathbone's now became. By the feeble light of the oil lamp, his features appeared twisted like that of one unmercifully condemned.

"Well, they've done it!" he exploded, beating one clenched fist against the air. "Those beasts—those demons—they've done it! They've had their way! Just look at their handiwork!"

With a sweeping gesture, he indicated the split and leaning houses.

For one wild terrible instant, the suspicion came to me that Rathbone's troubles had turned him stark mad.

"Listen, Steve," I expostulated, "you don't mean to say those mutineers could make an earthquake?"

"Those mutineers—those vile ruffians—those criminals—yes, they've made the earthquake!" he insisted, swinging one arm as if to pound someone. "They've done it deliberately—oh, it's abominable!"

"That's right," Norwood threw in. "This wasn't an ordinary earthquake. Those dirty curs did it, all right. The gaping imbeciles didn't know what they were doing."

"No, may God forgive them!" wailed Rathbone. "They thought they'd get revenge—take it out on the pit, which they blamed for all their troubles. I begged them not to—Lord, how I begged them—"

"You mean they told you about it?" I broke in.

"Yes, the filthy saboteurs! That brigand Scruggs phoned at 5.55 to cackle and crow about it. He said we hadn't accepted his ultimatum, so he'd given his orders. I cursed him then as I'd never cursed any man in all my life, but he cackled and crowed all the more. Said he wouldn't turn back if they blew up the whole island."

"But what could he have done, Steve?"

Rathbone took two or three strides in the snow; then pointed to the misty red light that was growing more pronounced in the eastern sky.

"Oh, it was all idiotically simple. Scruggs had the storerooms. The storerooms had hundreds of sticks of dynamite, which we kept for incidental blasting. What did that thug do but have them all brought to the top of the pit and dropped in at exactly six A.M.! Just imagine—"

He was interrupted by a shout from a little to our left. "Hey, look at the mountain!"

We all turned to gaze at Devil's Peak. The barest wisp of reddish vapor was curling above the summit. But at this sight, Rathbone uttered a shriek.

"Smoke! Smoke! Volcan—"

His sentence was never finished. A brilliant flash, bursting from the eastern plain like unusually bright lightning, interrupted him sharply. Instantly it was succeeded by other flashes, which catapulted heavenward like inverted shooting stars, or like comets with phosphorescent red tails, following one another with uncountable rapidity. At the same time, the earth once more heaved and quivered. A few seconds later, when the lights leapt with white and emerald flashes and blazing blue electrical flares, a rumbling and booming as of concussion bombs crashed upon our ears in a series of deep-toned detonations.

Then, after a minute that seemed packed with the doom of epochs, the tumult died down, the fiery spectacle waned. In place of the shooting tongues and streamers, a single glaring fountain jutted skyward, shaped like a mighty geyser, and sullen rose-red. It did not crash and rumble now, but hissed like escaping steam. And within a few minutes an acrid, sulphurous odor was blown to our nostrils; the air grew heavier and warmer; and red-hot ashes drifted to us across the wind. All over the eastern skies a ruddy glow began to rise.

For long moments we poor watchers, pressing together like trapped rats, could only stare at that fury above us with blind instinctive dread, while listening to nightmarish screams and yells from all over the settlement. I do not know how long it was before Norwood, swifter to recover than the rest of us, shouted the explanation.

"The pit! The pit! The fires come from the pit!"

Rathbone clutched my arm as though he needed its support.

"The pit! The pit! The fires come from the pit!"

From the watching crowd, in one tortured voice, there burst a low moan of dismay. Meanwhile Rathbone, half supported by my arm, covered his eyes with his hands. And all the time, in the distance, that red geyser still shot skyward, hissing continuously, belching sparks and fumes, spattering the sky with a crimson flame matched by the crimson trail of smoke that still rose like a slow menace above Devil's Peak.

XX

A roll call revealed that just thirty-nine of us were left. I was so stunned and shocked it was not surprising that I missed Rathbone's next words, and only picked up the thread at ". . . impossible situation. If the eruption dies down, maybe we can rebuild and pass the winter here. But if it grows worse"—a fresh roar from the direction of Devil's Peak made me miss several more words—"desperate last resource. Wouldn't recommend it under any other circumstances. . . ."

McDougal, at my left, coughed violently, making me miss another sentence or two. When I once more caught up with Rathbone, he was saying something about, "Wrangel Island, six or seven hundred miles south—terrific obstacles between, and as harsh a spot as you'd find, though we might get game enough to keep us for the winter, living in snow huts."

"How about the radio?" Allenham shouted. "Can't we radio for help?"

"The transmitter," answered Rathbone, "was in the powerhouse. And we had only one."

"But how can we cross the ice?" I demanded. "You know we've only two dog teams. These couldn't carry food for more than half a dozen of us, at most."

"I know," Rathbone shouted back glumly; "it's dangerous as the devil. But maybe no more so than staying here. However, have you forgotten my ice cruiser?"

I had indeed forgotten this tank-like machine, which Rathbone had built to traverse the ice.

"Didn't think of any such emergency when I made it," he went on, "but it could carry us at least to Wrangel. Tests have proved it can cross the roughest ice. Luckily, it's still in A-one condition."

He pointed to the shed at the settlement's western end, which contained the ice cruiser and the two large trailer sledges. Though the shed walls had burst apart, the contents were still whole.

A brief jarring of the earth intervened.

"Main trouble with the cruiser," Rathbone continued, "is that it's not big enough. Couldn't possibly carry us all, plus necessary provisions. Some of us will have to use the dog teams. But who will use which? Lord forbid that we'll have to use either."

As if to echo this sentiment, the dogs broke out in a particularly loud wailing. And the earth trembled once more, and its hollow depths gave forth a more portentous grumbling and roaring.

"Don't want to alarm you needlessly," Rathbone continued, his voice more strained than ever, "but let's be prepared. Let's load the cruiser and sledges. However, first let's have something to eat. We've got to conserve our strength."

Under Rathbone's control, we broke into a carton of chocolate and a pile of frozen meat. And after we had somewhat refreshed ourselves, we began to heap the remaining provisions upon the ice cruiser and the sledges.

The final blow came with shattering suddenness. Without warning, after a comparative lull, a wave of electricity shot through the air, shocking us all like a live wire, and knocking several of us to the ground. Terrorized, bewildered, hardly daring to speak, we regained our balance, only to hear a world-shaking blast, and to see torrents of earth and rock puffed high in air and falling in a fiery avalanche above the pit. At the same time, rocket bursts of flame were gushing from Devil's Peak, which by some horrible freak had changed shape, had suddenly become much lower.

At first we were too dazed to realize that the rim had been blown off. But we did know that red-hot rock and blazing liquid were cannonading through the air. We did hear a rumbling as of heavy artillery; we did see that the atmosphere was thick with dust and smoke; we did notice a glaring red patch on the side of Devil's Peak, rapidly expanding where boiling lava was galloping down the steep slopes.

While these sights flashed upon our eyes, a great crashing burst forth near at hand, accompanied by a hot wind and a fountain of flame. And where the ruins of one of the houses had been, suddenly there was only a red, hissing crater.

At the same instant a man, with violently swinging arms, rushed into our midst. His whole frame was shaking; his tormented eyes reflected the rose glow of the heavens.

"Get ready, everybody! Hitch up the dogs! Start the cruiser! Hurry! No time to lose!"

Several minutes later, the dog teams hitched, the

motor of the ice cruiser throbbing impatiently, the whole band of us pressed together into the open space before the settlement, where the softening snows were red with the light of the burning sky. Already we could see how the downrushing lava, penetrating the gorges at the base of Devil's Peak, was seething and hissing into Frost Lake, whose waters were rising in clouds of steam.

As the thirty-nine of us crowded there, some forcing their way into the ice cruiser and others fighting for a place in the sledges behind it, Rathbone by a mighty effort brought back relative order.

"Out of there, all of you!" his overstrained voice yelled at us. "If we're to come through, you'll have to do what I say!"

At this, some of the intruders voluntarily came out of the ice cruiser, and the rest were dragged and thrown out.

"Now we'll have to decide," Rathbone shouted, "who's to go on the dog teams!"

This was indeed a problem. Only six could accompany the dog teams—the maximum for which provisions could be carried—which would mean thirty-three to go with the ice cruiser, a capacity load.

"I hate to ask any of you to use the dog teams," Rathbone proclaimed, as he stood beside the laden sledges. "I myself will be one of the six—"

"Like fun you will!" Norwood cut him short. "Who'll lead the rest of the gang, and drive the ice cruiser?"

This question was unanswerable.

Now, unexpectedly, someone else volunteered.

"Me use dog team," announced Quin, scowling at the ugly gray hull of the ice cruiser. "I know best about dog team!"

"Me, too!" chimed in the other Eskimo dog driver.

Rathbone quickly nodded assent. But the rest of us stood by in a shuddering silence, unwilling to volunteer. The ice cruiser, which could make as much as fifteen miles an hour, offered a much brighter hope than the dog teams, which might not average fifteen miles a day.

"Four more names needed!" Rathbone hastily continued. "I'll not call for volunteers. Suppose we draw lots. Everyone willing?"

We all nodded.

"That is," he added, as his glance fell upon a slim figure who stood in the thick of the crowd, trying to smile through her tears, "we'll draw lots among the men."

"No, we won't!" Ada piped up briskly. "I've shared our risks from the start, I want no special favors now!"

Rathbone sighed wearily. "All right, Ada. We haven't time to argue."

Surely it was his utter fatigue that drew this concession from him. In the manner of a very tired man, he pulled a small notebook and pencil from an inner pocket, and (the air now being warm enough for an unmittened hand), tore out thirty-six sheets, left thirty-two blank, and marked four with crosses.·

"Those who pick the crosses go with the dog teams," he explained. "I'll shuffle."

For the moment, in our eager interest, we had forgotten the flame-vomiting skies, the smoke-clogged air, the wavering earth.

The first five to draw, including Norwood and myself, picked blanks. Allenham, the sixth, shook visibly as he plucked his bit of paper from Rathbone's closed hand—and fell back with a grunt of relief. McDougal, who followed, went pale as he stared at a cross. Thomas Whitney, two beyond, likewise started back from a cross as from his own death sentence. The next thirteen all drew blanks. Then "Art" Hogan took the third cross.

The following ten all chose blanks—which left only three to go, with one cross still unaccounted for.

With a pang of fear I glanced at Ada, as she stepped forward to pick one of the last three. Her hand did not waver, though her face blanched just a little as she held up a cross.

"Ada, Ada," I cried, starting forward in protest, "you can't do this! You, a woman, can't go by dog team! Come; we'll change places!"

She held her head up erect and proud. Her voice was firm. "No, Rodney, no! I've made my choice!"

"Ada, be reasonable!" Rathbone started to plead.

But she seemed not to hear. She was gazing at Allenham. He, however, turned his back and appeared absorbed in watching Devil's Peak.

"If you do go," I stormed, "I go with you! Here, you, Whitney! You don't want to take the dog team! Come; let's change places!"

Whitney muttered a vague protest, but his resistance was not too long or loud.

At the same time, Norwood was accosting Hogan. "Hey, Art, what you say to giving me your place? You know blasted well you'd be lost with a dog team!"

Hogan gripped Norwood's hand in a grateful clutch.

"Rather have a dog team any day than an ice cruiser," Norwood called into my ear. "Besides, we've been through a lot together, you and I, Rod— might as well stick it out to the end. Also, Ada may need me."

Amid the excitement of the departure, the fury of shouted orders, Rathbone nodded a quick assent to our change in plans, squeezed my hand eloquently, and called out in hurried farewell, "Take good care of Ada, Rod. Take good care of Ada. See you further along the road!"

An instant later, he had disappeared beyond the heavy glass door of the ice cruiser. With a whirring of motors and grinding of chains, the machine started jerking and bumping away, trailing the sledges with their fur-clad men. We caught just a glimpse of the sad, earnest face of Dr. Straub, the frightened face of Allenham, and Knowlson's face twisted with an agonized grimace. Shouts went up, barely heard amid the commotion of the elements; arms waved excitedly. Then the great lumbering vehicle passed behind a low ridge and out of sight.

I had never known anything quite like the feeling of loneliness, of desertion that now swept over me. We six humans, with hundreds of miles of icy barrens separating us from the nearest habitation, had only two dog teams and two sledge-loads of provisions between us and destruction.

But we had no time to contemplate or plight. The air was now so heated that the snow all about us was melting; those parts of the sea ice not cracked by the earthquake were splitting into fragments. Hence we had to cover the first few miles on land, pushing westward to where the ice remained intact. Silently, with blood-less faces, we followed the trail of the ice cruiser, walk-ing to save the dogs. We skirted crumbled headlands; we passed earthquake fissures, and miniature craters gouged out by red-hot volcanic stones; we waded through newly melted icy pools; we felt the earth jerk-ing beneath us, heard roars like the muffled beating of drums, and watched the pillar of flame above Devil's Peak, which resembled some Gargantuan tree-trunk that branched in a wide crimson cloud canopy.

About five miles from the settlement, the trail of the ice cruiser turned south along the snow-covered beach and across the frozen ocean. But as we set out into this frigid infinity, we felt more helplessly adrift than ever. I remember how I plucked at Ada's arm, just to reas-sure her; I remembered, too, how her wan smile flashed back at me from beneath glistening lids. At the same time, Norwood's shout came from the dog team just behind, "We're getting on fine!" Somehow, he made me think of a man whistling in the dark.

On and on, hour after hour, we trudged across the red-tinged ice and snow. Then, pausing to eat and sleep, we built our snow huts, and unharnessed and fed the dogs, while the blazing spout of Devil's Peak looked only a little more distant than before.

After eight hours we arose, much refreshed; and again plodded across that gray-white desolation, guided always by the tracks of the ice cruiser. That day we covered well over twenty miles. Yet when we made camp, the torrents of fire were still clearly visible: one over Devil's Peak, and one from the sparkling cone above the pit, now a secondary volcano of no mean size. Meanwhile fitful lightnings still knifed through the heavens.

As we once more threw up our snow huts, Ada startled us all with a cry and pointed to a sudden brightening in the fires, an ominous flaring of white and crimson lights. Incandescent showers, so bright that we had to shade our eyes, shot upward to the seeming level of the stars. At the same time, the surface beneath us began to heave as though billowed upward by some tremendous swell of the waters; with a terrifying booming and grinding, the ice began to crack.

Speechlessly we six pressed together. Almost immediately, a ruby streamer blazed from end to end of the heavens; coruscating white electrical balls, like St. Elmo's fire, danced and glittered at the zenith and halfway down to the horizon. Then came the most breathtaking spectacle of all. In an instant, the two flaming cones and the glaring red ridges of the island were blotted from sight and the skies were all a fury of sparks—blue and yellow darting sheets and stars and hurtling bloody firebrands, as though a thousand lightning bolts had mingled with a hundred thousand inverted meteors.

So brilliant was the sight that I thought of an atomic explosion all the more so since we could feel the atmosphere growing hot. Yet within a few minutes a tempestuous wind, summoned by the rise of heated air, began to blow from the south, cooling us as suddenly as we had been warmed, and saving our lives by solidifying the thawing ice.

It was minutes before, dizzy and bewildered, we could look steadily toward the north. And then low exclamations went up from us all, and we pointed—silently pointed.

From east to west, the skies were still glowing. But where were the two bright cones, the burning red ridges of the island?

As we stood there helpless, we guessed the truth we did not need to mention. Icy Isle had sunk beneath the sea!

XXI

If we had been a few miles nearer to the island, none of us would remain to tell the tale. Even as it was, we were imperiled by the cracking sea ice and the clouds of dust and suffocating vapors. Had we not plugged doggedly southward despite our exhaustion, our last hope would have ended.

A long nightmare followed. Day after day, day after day, we labored across never-ending ice fields, struggling around pressure ridges and leads of open water, always following the path of the ice cruiser. But during this bleak interval two events did occur, one fortunate, one tragic.

The fortunate event concerned the one woman in the party. During all those tormented days, amid the snow-drifts, the numbing winds and the darkness, Ada jogged along staunchly with the rest of us, never complaining, rarely seeking relief by riding on one of the sledges. Meanwhile even I, though schooled in misfortune, suffered horribly; often, while I struggled to hide the fact, I felt the effects of the lung impairment resulting from last year's illness.

Once in particular, at the end of the day's trail, my breath was coming in gasps, and there was such an aching around my heart that I threw myself down in the snow behind one of the sledges, hoping for a moment's rest where I could not be seen.

As I lay there, too wretched for words, I saw an approaching blubber lamp, and a pair of soft blue eyes stared down at me from beneath a fur hood. Even by the feeble light, the expression in those eyes was unmistakable.

"Ada," I whispered. And as I lifted myself to a sitting posture, somehow I felt much less miserable.

"Yes, Rodney," she said, with a tenderness I had never before heard from her lips.

"Ada, Ada dear—"

On an impulse as swift and uncontrollable as my own, she bent down and brushed my lips with hers. "Rodney, dear! There!"

She was about to dart away, but I seized her arm and drew her to me. "Ada, Ada darling! You know how

I feel—"

"Yes, Rodney. This isn't the time or place, but we both feel the same. Now come; conserve your strength, dearest. We'll talk about all this later."

I do not know from what unseen source I gathered energy. I rose to my feet; I started off at her side. But as I did so, a jealous thought clutched at me.

"Alan—Alan Allenham—" I started to say.

All at once the gentle light went out of her eyes. Her lips twitched. She drew herself up to her full height, and with an effort at self-control, requested, "You'll do me a favor, Rodney, if you never, never mention that man's name to me again!"

The second event occurred—or, rather, was discovered —a day or two later. We had been traveling across a hard, snowy surface by the light of a three quarters' moon; as usual, we had been following the ice cruiser's clearly marked trail. But all at once Norwood, trudging along with the dog team ahead of ours, let out a sharp cry. The rest of us could see him pointing in evident consternation.

Running to the borders of a narrow open lead, we saw how the trail of the ice cruiser had abruptly broken short. Neither to the right or left, nor on the snowy opposite bank, was there any trace of the heavy tracks!

All too quickly we took in the meaning. Then, like trapped men who clamor for a way out though they know there is none, we searched crazily on all sides. But there was not a clue, although we scoured both banks of the lead for hundreds of yards.

No wonder that now at last Ada broke down and sobbed. No wonder that McDougal threw up his arms as if imploring mercy of unseen gods; while even Norwood's craggy face showed the frozen traces of a tear. Every one of us, in his own way, had to confront the terrible truth: the ice cruiser, many times bulkier than the dog teams, had been too heavy for the thin ice at the rim of the lead; the surface had given way, plunging the cruiser and its passengers to the bottom of the sea.

By the dark, tomblike surface of that narrow lane of water, we stood together with bowed heads, offering up a prayer for the souls of our lost comrades, and above all for him who, indomitable even in defeat, had found a fitting resting place in the cold bosom of that North he had striven so valiantly to conquer.

Then, while the teardrops turned to ice on the cheeks of more than one of us and the rest of us looked on with set, dismal faces, we snapped the lashes once more above the dog teams. . . .

Seventeen days later, our food exhausted, half of our dogs dead from hunger and fatigue, we struggled in a spectral-cheeked band to the rocky coast of Wrangel Island, where a small colony of trappers found us, and warmed the life back into our frozen bodies.

From there, the following summer, we were flown to Nome; then promptly took passage for New York, where I sit writing these memoirs. As I click the keys of my typewriter, Ada is at my side, nodding to me with an occasional wifely word of admonition. Both of us, like our friend Norwood, hold that our story would have had a different ending had Rathbone chosen any spot but Icy Isle. The principles that guided him, we know, were sound; and some day, beneath the direction of some other man of vast energies and boundless resources, his experiment will be renewed elsewhere, and then at last the proud Arctic will yield to the genius of man, and the once frozen wastes offer food and habitation for earth's teeming millions.